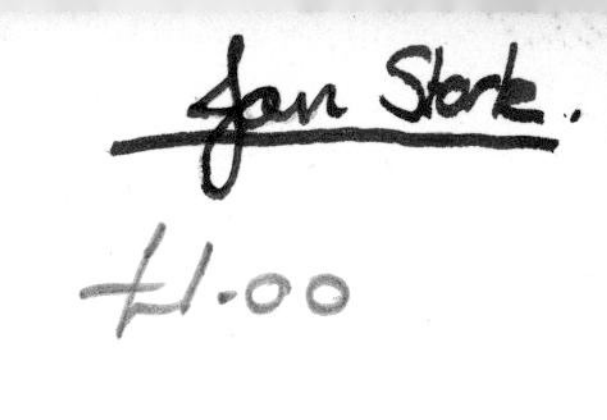
Jan Stark.
£1.00

D1393000

The CLOTH MERCHANT'S APPRENTICE

This book
is dedicated to
Viv, Tom,
Lesley and John,
with many
thanks

THE CLOTHMERCHANT'S APPRENTICE

Written and illustrated by
Nigel Suckling

The
first volume in
the tale of Rufus,
the clothmerchant's apprentice,
showing his early days and the beginning
of his acquaintance with the Golden Wheel

Big O Publishing, London

A Big O Original
First published in 1979 by **Big O Publishing Ltd**
219 Eversleigh Road London SW11 5UY
Telephone 01-228 3392 Telex 914549

American distribution by **Big O Publishing**
Box 6186 Charlottesville Virginia 22906
Telephone 804-977 3035 Telex 822438

ISBN 0 905664 08 6
Available in hardback. ISBN 0 905664 07 8

Printed in England by Butler & Tanner Limited

Contents

I The Beginning 7
II The Temple of Brown Gods 17
III An Unusual Table 25
IV Old Friends 32
V The Old Woman in Black 40
VI Four Visitors 49
VII The City of Brown Gods 57
VIII The Contest 70
IX The New King 78
X Aznavor's True Colours 88
XI The Golden Wheel 98
XII The Haunted Hills 107
XIII Strange Encounters 115
XIV Dreams that Stay Fully in the Mind 127
XV The King's First Judgement 139

—I—
The Beginning

THERE WAS once a great city. It sprawled over several low hills and burned like a pale brown jewel in the sunshine. As to where exactly this city was, its name and the time this history begins, unfortunately I know very little.

From its appearance it seems to me that the city was somewhere on the fringes of Asia Minor, some way north of Arabia because its winters were cooler.

As to time I can only guess that our story begins several hundred, if not a thousand or two, years ago.

Looking down over the city from a height you would see multitudes of domes and cupolas, flat or curved roofs mostly untiled and simply plastered like the building walls. You would see white, dusty courtyards and markets teeming with well-tanned folk in simple dress. Cypress trees here and there glow greenly against light-coloured walls and in windows pots of bright flowers peep out merrily.

Along one of the streets of this city strolled a young man named Rufus, tossing a pouch full of coins up and down with one hand. Beside the street ran a low wall and beyond the wall splashed a pleasant stream. Those with nothing in particular to do leaned over the wall, watching the water as they chatted and argued. Children sat dangling fishing lines hopefully into it or throwing in sticks and flowers to be carried away like ships.

Rufus noticed little of this as he strolled along. He was a trader, his head was full of numbers.

In another part of the city, in a dark and mysterious room, sat a completely different kind of person. He was gazing into a glowing crystal globe set before him on a little table. Within the globe tiny human shapes moved. He was gazing on a miniature street scene with tiny people going about their morning business. One of these turned off the street, crossed a little humped bridge, passing an old man struggling with arthritis, and disappeared into a dark alley. The watcher of this little scene sat back thoughtfully. He smiled a malicious smile to himself which bared all his stained teeth.

'Perfect,' he said aloud to himself, 'he most certainly is just what I've been looking for. Not too clever but also not too stupid; not too proud but proud enough; not particularly handsome but handsome enough; not too greedy, but he can be tempted all right. Best of all he's strong, honest and hasn't a whit of imagination at all. We'll have to put him to a few tests first, however.' In fact he was not being quite fair to Rufus, although there is a grain or two of truth in what he said.

Rufus walked along the dark alleyway, still lost in his calculations, till he was startled by a shower of rubble crashing to the ground a few paces ahead of him. He glanced up just in time to see a ragged figure scramble over the rooftop high above him. Some more rotten plaster was torn away by the bare, scrabbling feet and came tumbling down into the alley. A moment later a tousled head peeped over the edge of the roof to see what damage had been done.

If the alley had not been so empty the urchin would have been showered with curses, but Rufus simply shrugged his shoulders and walked on.

His thoughts turned away from business and drifted back a few years to when he was young enough to roam the rooftops freely. Most children in the city did this at some time in their lives, usually in gangs which were forever embroiled in wars and feuds and rivalries. The roofs were a different world from this adult world down on the streets, the only time adults went up there was on hot summer nights when they slept on the roofs to escape the stuffiness of their houses.

There was a third world too, beneath the streets in tunnels and passages and forgotten cellars, but few ventured down there.

These three worlds had one thing in common. Nearly all who grew up in the city barely thought or even believed in any world apart from them. The universe for most of them ended at the city walls. This was so despite the fact that most of their food and the goods which filled their many markets came from beyond the walls. Though they listened to the tales of travellers with interest, it was also with a strange disbelief as though they were listening to fairy stories. Few were tempted to leave their homes and venture out beyond the city gates. You had only to stand, as not many did, on the city wall and compare the exciting bustle behind you with the empty, arid waste out there to wonder at the madness of travellers.

Rufus had sometimes belonged to gangs as a child, sometimes not. He would never leave one for any particular reason, he'd just drift away and go off on his own. Even when he was a member of a gang there was something about him which kept him apart from the others, he was always a bit of an outsider. Nevertheless he was welcomed because of his great strength.

Rufus was vaguely dissatisfied with life. When at last he arrived at a market and came to his stall, his dissatisfaction increased. He was late today, having had to call on someone on the way to settle a deal. His father had already set up their stall and arranged the bright bales of cloth. They were cloth

merchants, he and his father. Or rather his father was the merchant and he the apprentice. His father nodded at him with no great warmth.

'Morning, son.'

'Morning, father.'

'You settled it, then?'

Rufus gave him the purse full of coins in reply. His father counted them and stowed them in a pocket in the front folds of his robe. That was the extent of their conversation until a while later when the father left with a murmured farewell and a vague wave of his hand. He was off to set up another stall at an afternoon market in a different quarter of the city. As Rufus watched him lead off the patient donkey and cart, his slight uneasiness nagged him again like an itch.

Why exactly Rufus was dissatisfied it's hard to say, certainly he himself wasn't clear about it. Part of it he knew was this business of becoming a merchant. He could feel it creeping into his blood gradually, the merchant's way of thinking, always totting up figures and weighing things in the balance and being friendly for the sake of business, growing every day more like his father and his father's father. Not that he held anything against his father—they got along well enough and rarely disagreed—there was just something stifling about the finality of it.

Looking up, Rufus noticed a troup of urchins swarming over a domed roof; shortly afterwards faint cries and yells drifted down to him over the market hubbub.

Business was not very brisk at his stall that morning and he did not feel up to crying his wares, so for much of the time he was left to his own thoughts.

He still went onto the roofs at times; in the evenings mostly when it was unlikely he would be noticed. He was eighteen then, rather past the age when such things were approved of. Soon, when he was running a larger share of the business, it would be still harder to escape. As it was the children who came across him sitting up there usually looked startled as if he was already a complete alien.

It wasn't quite that he wanted to go back to being an urchin or that he didn't want to grow up. When he saw youngsters scaling the heights he would sometimes feel a stab of envy, but also he pitied them because in a few years they would pass away like all the rest. They would be down on the ground plying some trade even if it was only as beggars. So Rufus did not want to go back to being a child, but if this was what growing older meant he didn't particularly want this either.

He thought to himself at times that there must be some other way, some people must find a way of growing old without losing the adventure of life. At times it seemed that his surroundings were becoming less and less clear, as if all these merchants' thoughts of deals and bargains were weaving a dusty veil around him. He could not see what to do about it. Rufus was not very imaginative.

'Where are you, lad?'

With a start Rufus lowered his gaze from a distant spire to the person who had addressed him.

'Far away were you, thinking of some young lady perhaps?' said the person.

It was a trader who had recently taken the stall beside Rufus'. He was pushing a handcart loaded with his goods. It was late in the day for someone to open a stall in this particular market; most business was usually done in the first few hours of the day. Rufus commented on this, not wishing to be impolite, but merely for something to say.

'The kind of customers I have will only just be taking breakfast,' said the other, 'that's if they're up at all. Don't you worry about me, lad, I know my business all right.' And he grinned up at Rufus with a dirty grin.

Although this was the longest conversation he had yet held with his neighbour, and so had very little to go by, Rufus instinctively disliked him. There was something rather hypocritical about his smile, something unpleasant about his rotten teeth. At the same time, however, Rufus felt attracted to him. He was strange. His goods were strange, too. Rufus watched as he set about unpacking.

He unpacked many little brown statues, some very graceful, some fearfully ugly. There were rich rosewood caskets inlaid with intricate patterns of gold. He hung a brass censer from the roof-frame and soon slender wreaths of smoke and a sweet pungent smell were spiralling out from his stall. Amongst china vases and mugs he set glass jars containing the oddest assortment of dried herbs and bits of animal; a jar of giants' teeth, another of dragons' teeth, several unlabelled bottles of powders and liquids, a fine brass quadrant, several water-pipes, magic amulets by the score, clay pipes, leeches' cups, astrological charts, pearls, rubies, rings, bracelets and a thousand other odds and ends, most of whose purposes Rufus could not even guess at.

Another unusual point about this trader was that he hardly tried at all to sell his goods. When he made a sale he treated it as if he was doing his customer a favour.

Because he both disliked this trader and yet felt interested in him, Rufus was rather afraid of him.

That day his neighbour was unusually talkative, not by the standards that anyone else would call talkative, but compared with the previous times Rufus had been next to him.

He was a short man, the trader. His robe was bright green, embroidered with curious yellow patterns. He was almost bald and as he leaned against the stall, gazing at the crowd, he chewed the root of some plant with his sharp, pointed, stained teeth. His eyes were like wolves' eyes.

That day, as he lounged like this, he would every now and then address himself to Rufus abruptly, with questions like:

'Have any brothers, lad, have you?' or:

'Ever seen the desert at night, boy?' or:

'Look as if you have a few drops of foreign blood in you; where from, your mother's side was it or your father's?'

These questions kept catching Rufus off guard. He found himself answering quite truthfully, before he had time to reflect or take offence at the other's curiosity and the way he kept calling him 'boy' or 'lad'. In this fashion the trader learned much of what Rufus knew about himself.

Rufus could not help him much with the history of his family though, as he knew very little himself. His mother was long dead and his father had never been one to talk about such things. A great many people in that city were the same. The city was so large it had swallowed up people of all nations, but most who stayed forgot their homes after a few generations; after all, the city was the universe. Not all did so as we shall see. Those groups who did not forget their homes and customs were not looked upon as real city folk, however. They were tolerated peacefully enough but they were outsiders, and little interest was taken in them. They added colour to the background of life though and were always good targets for a joke.

As the afternoon sun sank behind the taller buildings and the air began to cool, the trader started to pack away his goods. Others did the same but Rufus had to wait for his father and the donkey and they would be another hour at least.

It was a pleasant time of day, the stalls gradually emptying, the traders relaxing and bidding one another goodnight. Cool breezes blew welcomely from the shadows after the heat and dryness of the day. A few buyers wandered about casually, picking up bargains and cheap vegetables without the usual haggling. Dogs and children scavenged and played noisily among the heaps of refuse, their voices echoing more and more as the place emptied.

His neighbour left one article out as he fastened the bundle on his handcart. As he was leaving he pushed it roughly into Rufus' hand, saying, 'Here, this is for you; don't open it till after dinner this evening,' and went off without another word, pushing his squeaking handcart before him.

In Rufus' hand lay two objects, a little brass casket and a tiny key. The casket was engraved in the same curious, minute way as many of the trader's other goods. If he had not at that moment had a late customer, Rufus would probably have opened the box there and then, but as it was he put the box away in a pocket and the key into his money-pouch. By the time he had finally dealt with the lady, and made a surprisingly good sale, his father had arrived.

'Been doing business like that all day, have you, son?' said his father, eyeing the customer receding into the shadows with a satisfied smile.

''Fraid not, father, it's been a slow day today.'

'Not to worry, I've done well enough for both of us over at the other place.'

They packed up the stall and returned home.

Home for Rufus and his father was rather like living in a warehouse. It had once been a pleasant enough place. Its garden had had a high white wall around it. In the centre, in the middle of an emerald patch of grass, there had flourished a beautiful orange tree. Around the grass there had been bright beds of flowers, bushes of all kinds grew beside the paths and at the foot of the walls. In one corner there had been a seat shaded from the sun by thick vines. The garden had been filled with the gentle sound of white doves and tinkling from the wind-chimes in the windows of the house. A flight of stone steps, steep ones, led up to the house from the garden. In the old days both these and the house were always sparkling white.

With the passing of Rufus' mother the house had gradually become shabbier and shabbier. The house itself had become filled with bales of cloth while the garden had been turned over to the donkey. Only the orange tree had survived him and still grew, though rather mournfully. Everything else was mud and rubble. In one corner a clutter of grey bits of wood marked where the shady seat had been. The dovecote was lying shattered on the ground. If fell over one day when the donkey, having a fierce itch, rubbed himself too vigorously against its post. Now instead of doves it housed a thriving colony of mice.

Rufus and his father had not particularly noticed or regretted these changes except in so far as it was much more convenient to have things this way. It had happened so gradually they never felt they were doing any violence to the mother's memory. One day it would happen that the father was too tired to take his stock over to the warehouse, so it would be left in the house. Another day he would be too tired to take the donkey to its stable so it would be left in the garden. And so it went on until one day they wondered why they troubled themselves with a warehouse and stable at all when the house was big enough for all their needs.

So this was where Rufus and his father returned to that evening. It was dark and dusty inside, the windows only being opened on the hottest evenings, but they noticed it no more that night than any other. Between them they prepared and ate the meal, then sat by the cooking fire with a jug of wine apiece.

Then it was that Rufus remembered the little casket. All at once the laziness which usually crept over him at that time of evening left him. He didn't want to open it in front of his father, but neither did he leave the room just then. He sat and sipped his wine, staring into the flames and wondering about the strange trader.

Presently his father left the room. At once he took the little key from his pouch and the box from his pocket and held them near the lamp to see them more clearly. Like a child with a present he shook the box and examined it all over before opening it. It felt as though it was empty. Then he did open it, slowly. Inside there was nothing but a folded piece of paper. Just then his father returned, he quickly put the box back in his pocket.

Shortly afterwards Rufus went down into the garden. It was cool now, almost chilly. The donkey came out of his shelter beneath the stone steps and trotted up to him, snorting in a friendly way and twitching his ears.

'Hello, Ned, you're in a frisky mood tonight—still feeling the spring, are you? Poor creature, spring's almost gone and you haven't seen a field or found yourself a wife yet. There's not much chance you will, either. Are you happy, Ned, are you satisfied with your lot?' At that moment the donkey did in fact look very happy. Rufus was scratching him behind his ears which was his most itchy and inaccessible spot.

They went together over to where the light fell from a neighbour's window. Once again he took out the box and the note from within it. He read it with difficulty in the poor light, scratching the donkey's ears as he did so. The note said simply:

'The Temple of Brown Gods near the eastern gate. Be there tomorrow night.' It was signed 'Aznavor' and next to the signature was a strange sign.

In another part of the city, in a dark mysterious room, sat a man in a green and yellow cloak. He was gazing into a glowing crystal sphere set before him on a little table. In the crystal he could see a young man and a donkey standing in a dark garden and reading a note by the light of a neighbour's window. The mysterious man grinned even wider than before, baring all his sharp, stained teeth.

Rufus was not quite sure what to think of the message. To tell the truth he was slightly disappointed, he had expected the box to contain more than a piece of paper. Surely, he thought, the trader could have simply handed him the note. Why be so mysterious about it? Why put it in an expensive box and tell him not to open it till after dinner?

If Rufus hadn't acquired such a practical mind, he would have understood why. If the trader had simply handed him the note he would never have dreamt of doing what it said. The eastern gate was on the other side of the city. As it was Rufus found himself thinking such thoughts as:

'Is Aznavor the trader's name, then?' and:

'The city's full of temples. Does he expect me to go to all those near the eastern gate until I find the right one?' and:

'It could take all night simply to get there and find the place,' and although his everyday self thought the idea of going ridiculous, some other part of him was busy weighing up the problems.

When Rufus woke the following morning the idea seemed even more preposterous. Fancy expecting him to cross the city at night in search of some temple he was almost certain not to find; and on the strength of such a vague invitation as well!

The dim shaft of sunlight coming through his dusty window lit up the carefully wrapped bales of cloth piled from floor to ceiling. That, after all, was reality, those bales of cloth. He may not at times feel quite happy about becoming a cloth merchant, but that was the way of it. Everyone complained about their jobs. Temples had nothing to do with him, he had never been inside one in his life. Most people he knew hadn't either.

Nevertheless that day at the market he did make some enquiries. There was no sign of the trader who had given him the note, but he asked casual questions of others and in the end talked with one who knew something. He had not only heard of the Temple of Brown Gods but had seen it and told Rufus more or less where it was to be found. He said also that the people who worshipped there were even stranger than other religious folk. They would tell strangers nothing about their religion or their country, nor would they allow anyone not of their race into the temple.

Now, as we have seen, Rufus as a true native of the city had never been particularly interested in religion, nor in the countries which some called their homelands, but he knew well enough that those who clung to such things were usually only too willing to talk about them when pressed.

As the day drew on towards that pleasant hour when market stalls were packed away for another night, Rufus began to change his mind about not going. More and more he wondered why it should be out of the question to make the journey that night. The tedium of the day may have had something to do with it. It seemed to him that all his customers that day were doing their best to annoy or cheat or insult him. The sun seemed to be doing its best to parch him although it was barely summer yet. Even the dogs were against him. They persistently came and peed against his stall.

By the time the shadows were lengthening and cool breezes starting to blow, the only reason Rufus could think of for not going was that he felt tired.

After dinner he told his father he was going for a walk and left the house.

It was a cool, starry night. The gentle breeze blew all the day's weariness out of him like dust. The bright, nearly full moon shone in the east as though beckoning him on. He could only see it now and then though, through gaps in the tall buildings. It was this that made him realise that of course the easiest way to cover such a distance would be across the rooftops.

With a thrill of pleasure running through his veins he looked quickly around; there was no-one to see him so the next moment he was scaling the high, rough wall beside him. When he reached the top his muscles tingled with the effort and at the same time slightly ached; he had grown rather flabby recently. Looking back on that moment afterwards, he realised that he experienced then the first real joy he had felt for years. He felt both young and old, he had the roofs to himself, a world to himself. He was strong and the moon and stars smiled down on him. The unknown lay ahead of him and at that moment he did not care at all that when he reached the temple he would probably be disappointed. After all, hadn't he been told they only allowed people of their own race to enter? Yet the trip felt worth it, simply for this freedom of the roofs at night. He wondered why he had never thought before of roaming them at night, why when he had visited them it had only been to sit and look out over the city, reflecting on his lost freedom. But then, as we have seen, Rufus did not have much imagination.

He bounded off over the roofs like a young lion.

—II—
The Temple of Brown Gods

WHEN RUFUS reached the eastern quarter of the city it did not take long to find the temple. His first glimpse of it was in the distance, mostly hidden by other buildings; but just that glimpse sent a pang of recognition through him as if he had known it all his life. He could imagine no other place which could be called the Temple of Brown Gods so fittingly. Even at that distance and in the moonlight he could see it was carved from head to foot with statues of gods; even in the moonlight he could see it was all raw stone.

The moon was near its zenith when he reached the rooftops overlooking the temple. He gazed on it in awe. The great dome in the centre and the four spires seemed alive with writhing carved figures, figures of all sizes from gigantic to minuscule, figures of all kinds from the grotesque to those with unearthly beauty. They reminded him of the statues the strange trader sold. Even the beautiful statues had a wild, almost threatening attitude, however, and if he had been asked to sum up the temple in one word he would probably have said barbaric.

The temple was set in a square of its own with a walled-in space between it and the neighbouring buildings. A large crowd bearing bright, multi-coloured lanterns was jostling through the gates into the square and filing into the temple. As Rufus was looking down on the scene, the tail-end of the procession came into sight. He realised there was no time to waste and hastily made to climb down from his perch.

By the time he joined the crowd the last of them were through the gates but there was still a fair number in the square waiting to enter the temple.

As he caught his breath and cooled down from his efforts, Rufus began to feel more and more conspicuous. The people he mingled with were all brightly dressed in clean, ankle-length robes whereas he was wearing only his plain, short jacket and was rather grubby from the journey. Even in the lantern-light the dirt showed and he looked more like one of the beggars who lined the temple steps than one who was intent on entering it. He pushed forward so as not to be at the end of the procession.

The robes of those around him were patterned in the same unusual way as that of the strange trader, Aznavor. Several of them cast suspicious looks on him, but they said nothing nor made any move towards him. Rufus soon saw why.

Just inside the great temple doors the crowd had to file past rows of fierce-looking guards who scrutinised each face closely, occasionally stopping one and demanding identification. Fortunately Rufus had had enough imagination to bring with him the brass casket and its message, or his story may never have come to be written down at all.

He took the box from his pocket and the message from within and held them tightly in readiness. His heart began to thump loudly.

When he passed through the great doors several things happened. The first guard in line, who was clearly the captain, whispered orders to his men. Some of these came around Rufus and held back that part of the procession behind him. The others, after carefully examining each person immediately before him, hustled them on into the temple and turned to form a wall with their bodies. Then one guard behind pushed Rufus firmly through the doors into the space beyond and the others closed around him in a formidable ring of leather and steel. Only then did anyone address him. The captain stepped into the ring and said:

'Well, well, and what do we have here? I hope you have a good reason for coming in like this, young man.'

Now, Rufus was not a person to be easily intimidated, and not even this captain would have worried him overmuch if they had met ordinarily; but it must be admitted that surrounded as he was by armed guards, in a temple of all places, with no way back and having come on only the most dubious of invitations, he could not have said a word just then even if he had tried. His throat was as dry as old parchment. Dumbly he held out the note given him by the trader Aznavor.

The captain took and read it. As he did so his face grew puzzled. He moved aside and showed it to one of his juniors. The other guard began to mutter and shrug—Rufus gathered it was because he couldn't read—but then he stopped sharply, took the note and examined it closely. The two held a whispered conference, glancing every now and then at Rufus with an expression he couldn't put a name to. He gathered, however, that it was the curious sign next to Aznavor's name which had disturbed them. The second guard went off somewhere and the captain came back to Rufus.

'Well it seems you may have a good reason after all, lad, though I doubt if I'll hear what it is. Will you come this way till we have you checked out?' So saying he led Rufus off to the side, at the same time signalling the guards to let in the last of the procession who were then pressing hard against their backs and peering over their shoulders to see what was going on.

The captain led Rufus to a small, bare chamber where they waited in silence. Every now and then the captain would give him a speculative glance but he seemed to come to no conclusion. Rufus began to feel he really was in for an adventure though what it might be he hadn't the faintest idea.

After a while the other guard returned. He and the captain held another whispered conference, then the captain said to Rufus:

'Well, it seems you're genuine enough whoever it is you're meant to be, but the first thing we have to do is change your clothes and clean you up a bit. If you'll go with our friend here, indicating the other with his thumb, he'll fix you up with all you need.' The captain left and Rufus was led away by the other guard.

They followed various narrow passages and winding stairs tunnelling upwards through the temple walls. Some of the windows they passed looked down in into the temple, others looked out onto the city through clusters of brown gods. They arrived at some chambers. The door was solid and there were no windows, reminding Rufus rather of a prison. Otherwise the chambers were pleasant enough, with comfortable furniture and rich hangings over the bare stone walls. In one corner was a steaming bath.

Rufus undressed and washed. His dirty clothes were put on one side and fresh ones brought. He was given a full-length robe like those worn in the procession, purple, with yellow designs on it. It was made from the purest silk which, being a cloth merchant, Rufus fully appreciated.

When he was washed and dressed the guard led him off again along more passages until, passing through a low door, they found themselves on a balcony high in the temple wall, looking down on the crowd. Rufus leant his elbows on the balcony wall and surveyed the scene below. The guard stationed himself beside the door, not having spoken a word all the time.

Since he had never, as far as he could remember, been to any kind of religious ceremony before, Rufus could make very little sense of what was going on below. Whatever it was, though, it seemed to be already in full swing.

Most of the crowd were gathered beneath the great dome, on the main floor of the place which was a few steps below the level of the entrance. The temple had many other levels though and the crowd was dispersed throughout these. Four great arched halls opened off the central space. In one of these, dwarfing everything else and with its head almost touching the roof, sat a giant brown rock statue. It smiled sleepily and kindly down on the noisy crowd as they swayed to some wild chant.

'That must be their chief god,' thought Rufus. It struck him how different it was to the other statues he had seen; it had none of their barbaric air. The chief god sat cross-legged like a tailor or cobbler. His figure was plump and rounded, making him appear almost feminine.

There were far less of the other statues inside the temple than outside, but there were still a fair number in niches here and there. Part of what Rufus disliked about them was that there seemed to be no distinction between the beautiful and ugly. A nymph might have her arms around the shoulders of a scowling goblin, yet still she smiled. Part of it was also, as he had noticed outside, that even the beautiful statues had a wild and threatening air.

'It's as well I don't believe in such nonsense,' thought Rufus, reflecting on this and on the chanting crowd. The crowd was falling more and more under the spell of their religious emotions and was swaying and revolving like a huge multicoloured whirlpool.

Although, apart from the giant one, Rufus did not much like the brown statues in the temple, he could not help admiring everything else he saw there. The walls and the inside of the great dome were brilliantly decorated with the most glorious tiles and mosaics he had seen. They climbed up the walls in bright, intricate patterns, set off here and there by plain areas of white or blue, leading to a dizzying blue pattern spiralling up the inside of the dome to its highest point where a white light burned steadily like a star.

By the time his eyes reached this point of light, Rufus was in a trance. The chanting and colours and heady incense had crept up on him so subtly he was not even aware of what had happened to him. He remained as he was, his head craned upwards and his eyes fixed on the point of light; like a statue himself except that his body swayed slightly from side to side in time with the chanting.

The only people in the place who seemed unmoved by all that was going on were the guards. How they managed it I have no idea.

After an immeasurable time, Rufus was brought back to his senses by a strident blaring of trumpets. A hush fell on the crowd. As the last echoes of the fanfare died away, all were in complete silence. All heads turned to face the towering brown god. Rufus turned his gaze in that direction also.

Onto a small balcony, just beside the giant statue's head, stepped a small figure. The figure was dressed in a green robe with yellow designs. It was none other than Aznavor, purveyor of curious objects and magical charms.

Rufus found it difficult to believe his eyes. Aznavor proceeded to deliver a speech, his voice echoing in the hall behind him and booming out to fill the temple. His voice was remarkably loud although he did not appear to be shouting, and it sounded different to the harsh, rasping voice Rufus knew. The little man sounded quite impressive.

For some reason he could make little sense of what was being said. Perhaps it was the strange accoustics of the place or perhaps Aznavor was speaking partly in some foreign tongue; whichever it was, Rufus was baffled and could understand only a part of the speech.

All he had learned by the end was that this festival was the beginning of the people's preparations for the crowning of their new king, the king of their homeland. They were praying to ensure that he would be a wise and just ruler. The idea that what they were doing in the temple that night could affect the matter either way seemed very strange to Rufus.

As Aznavor left the balcony there rose from the crowd a mighty roar which tailed off into a chant as they resumed their ceremonies.

Rufus was very puzzled. First of all by the high position Aznavor seemed to hold among these people, though outside in the city he was no more than a common trader. A rather peculiar trader, admittedly, but no-one special. Secondly it puzzled him that these people should be so involved in the affairs of some distant country. How would it affect them either way if the king was good or bad?

It seemed curious to him that over the next few weeks, or however long it was till the crowning, these people would presumably be carrying on their normal lives with no outward change, yet all that time their thoughts would be in that distant place.

'And where,' thought Rufus, 'do I fit into all this?'

He leaned on his balcony wall musing and wondering in this way, while the effects of the temple crept up on him again. This time, though, instead of going into a trance, he simply fell asleep, crumpling into a heap on the floor.

'Wake up, sir, it's time to go.'

Rufus woke to find the guard shaking him by the shoulder. Behind his stony expression the man seemed faintly amused.

'It's time for you to leave, sir.'

Rufus rubbed his eyes and stretched his cramped limbs. The temple was dim and empty save for a few guards and attendants clearing up. Most of the lamps and torches had been extinguished and the dim blue light of dawn filtered in through the open doors. A chill breeze was cutting through the smoky temple air.

Rufus shivered.

'Is Aznavor still here?' he asked.

'The lord Aznavor left some time ago,' replied the guard.

'Didn't he want to see me?'

'He said nothing about it, sir. He only said when he heard you were asleep that I should wake you when everyone had left and show you out, nothing more.'

'How strange.'

'If you will follow me, sir, I'll take you back to where you left your own clothes.'

So saying, the guard led him off to the room where he had changed earlier, provided him with a light breakfast and, when he was ready, led him down to the temple door.

When he stepped outside it seemed to Rufus, who was still drowsy, that he was stepping into some enchanted underwater scene. The dawn air was dark blue and chill, the shadows deep and the city silent save for the birds. The birds in waking were rousing each other with a mounting chorus of song, their calls echoed from the silent buildings. Here and there were a few warm yellow lights in windows, early risers setting about their breakfast.

'Should be a fine day today,' said the guard, who seemed to have taken quite a liking to Rufus since waking him. 'I hope you've recovered, sir; a bit strong for you last night, was it? If you don't mind my saying so you didn't look like you were used to this sort of thing.'

'Do you get used to it after a while, then?' asked Rufus.

'Well, in a manner of speaking, sir, but them that take part in it get accustomed in a different manner to us guards. We guards get accustomed so's it doesn't affect us hardly at all, we have to be alert in case of trouble, see.'

Rufus was about to leave but paused a moment and asked the man: 'It's strange, don't you think, that I should be asked all the way from the other side of town by Aznavor but that when I'm here he doesn't want to see me?'

'I wouldn't know anything about such matters, sir; it's a bit beyond my call of duty so to speak.'

'Well, I'll be off,' said Rufus. 'Thanks for the breakfast.'

'It was a pleasure, sir.'

Rufus went down the steps and out through the gate.

'It's also strange,' he thought to himself, 'that the guard should be so friendly to me this morning and call me "sir" all the time.'

Even though it would soon be daylight, Rufus climbed back onto the roofs and set off home the way he had come. He was full of the strangest assortment of moods. Not being used to examining his feelings very closely, he tried to distract his attention from them by tackling the most difficult climbs in sight. He was only partly successful, however.

Not least of the feelings he was trying to ignore was his disappointment. What exactly there was to be disappointed about he was not sure since the night had been stranger and more eventful than he had expected, but it may have been that once inside the temple his idea of the adventure he was involved in had grown somewhat, and he was disappointed now at being turned out with no hint of anything to follow. It may have been this but Rufus did not get so far as guessing it. He simply felt let down now his adventure was over. In this he couldn't have been more wrong, for in fact it had barely begun.

He also felt disappointed with himself for falling asleep, feeling it may have had something to do with this anticlimax.

'The devil take it,' he kept saying to himself aloud. 'I don't want to be involved in such superstitions anyway.' But each time he said this the flat, dreary expanse of days spent in market-places yawned before him like a yellow desert, a desert where you never starved or felt thirsty but just kept on walking through bright emptiness.

Last night had given him a taste of dark mystery.

He kept to the roofs until he was almost in his own neighbourhood. Even though the sun was high and the streets full of people who might see him, he could not face climbing down yet. It was as if in doing so he would lose something.

His feelings almost proved fatal to him. They drove him to follow paths he'd used in his most nimble and daring urchin days. As he was stepping onto a roof, one of the rare tiled ones, someone called him. A lad not far away was basking in the sun, lying against a dome, but he was waving frantically at Rufus and shouting something he couldn't understand. Rufus hesitated, and as he hesitated the roof under his right foot trembled and collapsed into the empty shell of the house below.

Shaken, Rufus waved his thanks and climbed down to the street to walk the short way home.

—III—
An Unusual Table

WHEN HE arrived home, Rufus found the house empty as was to be expected. His father had gone to market, leaving a note to say where he could be found. His father said nothing else in the note. Rufus was not sure whether to take this as a good or bad sign. He felt guilty himself at having slipped away without warning and his father was sure to be angry. If he had to have a telling-off, he'd prefer to have it now in a letter than later face to face.

At first he could not decide what to do that day. His body felt tired and in need of sleep, but his spirit was restless. After some refreshment, a wash and a change of clothes, he decided to go out, heading in the direction of the market his father had named.

On the way he changed his mind and made instead for the market where he usually worked, the one where he had met Aznavor. It was only a faint hope that led him there, so he was not much disappointed to find Aznavor's stall vacant. He decided he may as well face his father and get it over with, so he set off again in that direction.

It was mid-afternoon when Rufus reached the place. When his father saw him coming he made no greeting but stooped again over his work. He was wrapping a bundle of fine cloth in a piece of scrap linen. Only when his son had stopped beside him did he look up. For some reason he would not look Rufus in the eye.

'Afternoon, son.'

'Hello, father.'

'Wondered where you'd got to last night.'

'I had to see someone, it took a bit longer than I expected.'

'Thought something might have happened to you.'

'Oh, no, nothing happened, it just took longer than I expected.'

'A friend was it you went to see?'

'Not a friend, really, just someone I met. No-one you know, I don't think.'

His father grunted and bent over his parcel again. Rufus may have seen the hurt in his expression, but if so he certainly did not recognise it for what it was. He was rather surprised at his father's mildness.

'Haven't been out drinking, have you?' asked his father with a slight quickening in his tone.

'No, of course not. You know I never drink more than a jug after dinner. I tell you I just went to see someone.'

There followed a pause during which his father worked busily on his parcel. He had wrapped and unwrapped it at least three times since Rufus had arrived. It was clear he had something in mind but could not find the words. At last he burst out in exasperation:

'Well, it's hardly worth you starting now, is it? Get along with you, you might as well take the rest of the day off!'

'I'll finish off here for you if you like,' offered Rufus half-heartedly, but his father just waved him away without looking up. Undecidedly Rufus hung on a bit, patting Ned, who looked most bewildered. There seemed to be nothing to add to the conversation, however, so he turned and left.

For a few minutes he puzzled over his father's behaviour as he walked off. He felt his father had lost some kind of hold over him, which gave him a pleasant sense of freedom. He almost went as far as realising that he had hurt his father's feelings, but before reaching that point he dismissed the entire conversation from his mind with relief that it had passed off so easily. This was natural enough, for what son of eighteen, who has yet to leave home, ever imagines he need worry about hurting his father's feelings? His thoughts turned instead to the events of the previous night.

Next morning Rufus set up his stall as usual. His father led the patient donkey away as usual to some other market. Everything seemed to be as usual, nothing passed between them to show their relationship had changed, but each knew it had. The father more so than Rufus, who just felt he had somehow gained a little more independence.

Although annoyed with himself for doing so, Rufus spent most of the day wishing Aznavor would turn up. The stall beside his, however, was occupied by a parrot-seller whose wares did nothing to soothe Rufus' nerves. The parrots squawked and screeched all day, or repeated silly phrases endlessly. As if that wasn't bad enough, they kept flapping their wings and scattering seed and feathers over his bales despite the screen between the two stalls. By mid-afternoon Rufus had an aching head and short temper; the light hurt his eyes and he was almost turning customers away by his rudeness.

Even in the late afternoon he still had a faint hope that if Aznavor himself was not going to appear, there might be some message from him. There was neither sight nor sign of him, however.

The following day Rufus could not face work and told his father he was taking the day off. His father accepted the information in glum silence and went off into the morning alone, looking tired.

Rufus went out walking.

Through the city there flowed a fair sized river. When the city had been no more than a small town, the river was then no more than a stream which rose in one of the hills and trickled away to the edge of the plateau over which the city now sprawled. As the city had grown, however, more and more similar streams were diverted into this one until it had swollen to its present size. This river divided the city almost in half. It rose in one of the western hills and meandered eastwards until it left through an arched, bridge-like gap in the city wall, a mile or so north of the eastern gate. By the time it left the city, the river was a couple of hundred yards wide. It poured over the plateau's edge in a magnificent waterfall which a few of the more adventurous city-folk occasionally visited. Not many did so for reasons we have already seen; in fact the waterfall was more famous outside the city than within it. Amongst many travellers the town was known only as 'the waterfall city' because, after journeying across the arid, stony plain, that glistening column of falling water, with spray rising like clouds from its foot, was the first sign of comfort and rest at hand.

It was in the direction of this river that Rufus headed.

As he approached it, he found himself in a sad, derelict area. Most of the buildings there had either been gutted by fire or fallen into ruin. Those that were left more or less intact were either occupied by the poorest of people or used as warehouses, in whose grounds roamed packs of fierce, blood-thirsty mastiffs. The district grew more and more dismal the closer Rufus came to the river. The last stage of his walk was through dark, narrow alleys in an area that seemed completely deserted.

At last he came to the river. It was clean and sparkling in the sunlight; strong, smooth-flowing and hardly ruffled by wind. On the far bank, tethered boats bobbed up and down at their moorings, in mid-stream was some light traffic of small vessels. In contrast to the buildings on his side, those on the opposite bank were fresh and whole, full of light reflected from the water.

Between Rufus and the riverbank, and a little way to his left, stood a small, burnt-out temple. It was not a particularly attractive building but Rufus, with his interest in such things having been awakened, paused and drew closer to examine it.

It was a low squarish building set in a small area enclosed by iron railings. To me it seems like a poor example of Roman work but Rufus, knowing nothing of such matters, simply thought it rather ugly; squat and graceless, with heavy, square lines. Being blackened by fire probably did not help its appearance but it was not as badly damaged as it first seemed. The doors hung crookedly ajar but were more or less whole, the walls and roof had only crumbled in a few places.

Idly Rufus examined it for statues, thinking he might rescue any interesting ones from the ruin. This in itself showed that quite a change had taken place in him; he had never felt any such interest before. There was not much carving on the building, however; what there was simply being of urns and vases and heavy, graceless wreaths of flowers. Despite its unattractiveness, Rufus lingered outside the rusty iron fence. He would probably have gone to take a look inside the place if he had not at that moment become aware that he was not alone. Hearing voices, he turned.

Behind him was a dark, hollow space where no sunlight found its way. The roof and two walls of the space were formed by the ruined building above, the other two sides were open apart from a few rough, square pillars. One of these open sides faced the temple, the other the river. From within this dark space came the voices.

The first thing Rufus noticed as he looked in was a fire burning in the far corner. It was burning under a chimney which led up into the ruin above. Around it was an ornate grate of cast iron and coloured tiles which had clearly been salvaged from some grand, but now derelict house.

Then, as his eyes grew accustomed to the gloom, he made out the most curious collection of men he had ever seen, sitting around the fire on broken chairs. Accustomed as he was to seeing queer folk around the city, he could not remember seeing any as strange as these people. They were a villainous looking group. Rufus had a feeling that they only went abroad at night. They seemed to be discussing him, whispering and glancing in his direction. There was no threat in their faces, however, so Rufus stood his ground to see what would happen. Eventually one of them rose and came over towards him, stopping in the shadow behind a pillar.

'Good afternoon, fine sir,' he called. 'Will you do me the honour, sir, of allowing me to introduce myself. My name is Grogul, sir, at your service.'

He performed a kind of half-bow, holding out a rough, horny hand towards Rufus as he did so. Rufus walked over to him and shook the hand warily.

Although no taller than Rufus, Grogul looked massive beside him. He was built like a rock. His head looked as though someone had roughly chipped out the features with a hammer and left the job unfinished.

'You may be wondering, sir,' said Grogul, 'what service it is we're offering you. But you'll not be left wondering for long on that point I can assure you because I'm about to enlighten you.' Someone in the darkness tittered, but stifled the sound when Grogul turned a threatening glare in his direction.

'It's not often we have the honour of such company down here, sir,' he resumed, 'and some of us'—here he glared at the offender again—'have forgotten, if they ever knew, how business is conducted between gentlemen. Though I would not be so vain as to call myself a gentleman, at least, sir, you may be reassured that I know how to behave like one. Well, as I was saying, my friends and I, when we saw you standing there admiring that fine relic of past glory, well we could see at once you were a gentleman of taste and distinction. We could see you were a man of culture with a nose for a fine work of art and—well, to be brief, sir, it happens that we have here such a fine piece of work in which you may perhaps be interested. In short, sir, we have a proposition to put to you. I can see the interest in your eyes already, sir, I can see your nose has sniffed a fine bargain in the air. If you will do us the kindness of stepping this way, sir, I'm sure your curiosity will be well rewarded.'

Rufus stepped forward into the darkness, curious in spite of himself to see what they were talking about. He was very much on his guard, however, and ready to fly at the first hint of trouble. None of the others moved from their seats though and Grogul did not seem to be trying to get behind him. He felt safe enough.

When he entered the shadow he understood the need for the fire in the corner. For some reason the air in the hole was very cold and clammy. He hesitated just beyond the pillar to accustom his eyes to the dark. Seeing this, Grogul barked out:

'Hey, Lam! Bring a light here for the gentleman! Where's your manners?'

A spidery little fellow jumped up, lit a broken lantern from the fire, delivered it to Rufus and scuttled back to his seat. Grogul, keeping up his curious monologue all the while, led Rufus through the dark to one side and presented him with the object of his proposition. All Rufus could see was an old table with a pile of small articles on it. The table was dusty and had been scorched by fire.

'I must admit, sir,' said Grogul, 'that some slight damage has befallen this fine table, but take your time, sir, don't judge too hastily. Consider carefully before you make a decision. Look closer, you'd have to go far to find such craftsmanship again. Here's a bargain such as a gentleman rarely has a chance of. As to the damage, why an hour or two's work will see it as good as new. Hold the light closer, sir, so's you can see it clearly.'

Rufus did as he was told, though he kept a wary eye on the ruffians as he did so. He found to his surprise that he had been told the truth; the table really was a marvellous piece of work. Its top was carved with a strange pattern of circles set in squares, the finest work though was in the legs. There the solid wood had been carved into slender, intertwining, vine-like shapes which at first seemed too fragile to be of much use, but when he tried to rock the table he found it to be perfectly firm. The fire damage was only a scorching of the surface and the wood required only a rubbing down and a good coat of oil to restore it.

'One silver crown, sir,' said Grogul, 'is all the price we're asking for this fine piece of work. Of course we could fix it ourselves and sell it to some merchant for ten times the price, but for doing us the honour of visiting us here, and seeing we're all agreed you're a gentleman of distinction, it's yours, sir, for one silver piece.'

Rufus was now in a bit of a dilemma, never having bought anything like this before simply for its beauty. He could see no practical sense in it, but the table attracted him strangely. One silver piece did not seem much to spend on a whim, though it was a suspiciously low price for them to ask.

'I suppose it must be stolen,' he thought, 'but what harm would it do to buy it. If I don't it may well end up on that fire.'

He did not forget himself completely, however; his practical mind quickly raised one obvious objection. If he did buy it, how on earth was he to get it home? He had three crowns on him but he had come a long way that day. The table would require a large cart to carry it and that was likely to cost more than he had on him. It was also unlikely that in this part of the city he could find a carter to carry it home for him on credit.

The sensible thing to do was probably to buy the table, take it as far as he could with his money, and then decide what to do. That is, if he was sure that he wanted it that much—but that was exactly what he was not sure of. If he had been offered it in the street by his house he would have been ready enough to take it at their price, but this extra expense and trouble changed matters.

Grogul understood Rufus' hesitation to mean that the price was too high because he said slightly exasperatedly:

'I tell you what, sir, since I can see you're weighing matters very careful, as is only sensible for a businessman like yourself, I can see you drive a shrewd bargain so I tell you what we'll do; those fine trinkets there on the table which we were going to keep, those trinkets we'll throw into the bargain for nothing. Now we couldn't be more fair than that, could we? Not without giving it away for nothing.'

The little pile on the table was an assortment of curious junk, amongst which were a number of small black boxes. Rufus picked out one of these and opened it. Inside was a beautiful amethyst and clear crystal cross. The cross had arms of equal length and the stones twinkled even in that dim light. He looked in the other boxes. They too contained amethyst and crystal jewels, though none as fine as the first he had seen.

Now these gems made it more of a business which Rufus could weigh up practically since they were likely to fetch a price which would almost cover the costs involved. But still he could not bring himself to decide. He had the uncomfortable feeling of being at odds with himself. What did he want the table for? It was certainly attractive but it was hardly a practical thing, the pattern was so deeply incised on the surface as to make it almost useless. And was he really prepared to do the work necessary to restore it to its original condition?

'I tell you what, sir,' said Grogul persistently. 'You name any place within ten minutes' walk and we'll carry it there for you. Now you couldn't ask for anything more than that, could you?'

Rufus now grew slightly puzzled at their eagerness to sell all this to him for such a low price. Villains as they obviously were, he would have expected them to squeeze as much out of him as possible. He supposed, though, that perhaps being outcasts gave money a different value to them.

'You couldn't take it any further than that, could you?' he asked hopefully.

'Oh no, sir. We don't like to go too far from home, you know. Home-loving people we are, peaceful home-loving folk. You can't tell what wickedness you'd find abroad in the city. Isn't that right, lads?' Those sitting around the fire sniggered.

Then Rufus remembered passing a coffee-house on the borders of the derelict area. The place had a garden where people sat smoking and drinking sweet black coffee as they passed the time of day.

'I tell you what,' said Rufus, 'I have to get the money and arrange some transport in case I do decide to buy. If you can take it to . . .'—and he described the coffee-house—'I'll meet you there in about two hours. I'll be able to see it properly there in the open and come to a decision.' Even though he did not feel in any great danger, Rufus thought it best not to let them know he had any money on him.

Grogul, Lam and the others went into conference. There seemed at first to be some disagreement, for there was much shaking of heads and annoyance. Finally, however, they all seemed to more or less give their consent.

'It's agreed, young sir,' said Grogul, returning to Rufus. 'We shall meet you at the place you have so clearly described in two hours, give or take half an hour or so, complete with table and the contents thereof, there to await your decision. I have no doubt, sir, that with your fine judgement . . .'—Grogul went on like this for quite a while until Rufus finally managed to escape.

He walked back the way he had come, puzzling over what to do.

—IV—
Old Friends

SHORTLY AFTER this encounter, Rufus was passing a warehouse when a voice called out:

'Hey, Rufus! Hang on there a moment.'

A young man who had been talking to some workmen within the warehouse waved and hurried over towards him. After a few moments Rufus recognised him. It was an old acquaintance from the roof-scrambling days. In fact they had been together in their last gang before growing out of childhood. His name was Maro. He had changed much in the three or four years since they had been friends. He looked older than Rufus, more mature, prosperous and plump.

'Hello, old friend,' said Maro, coming up and shaking his hand. 'I thought for a bit that you were just going to pass me by. Do you ignore all your old friends nowadays?'

'No, of course not,' Rufus replied. 'I was just thinking about something and not looking where I was going. You look well, Maro, what are you doing with yourself these days?'

'In the cloth trade, old friend, and you?'

'The same.'

'Oh, yes, I remember now, our fathers were in the same business, weren't they? How do you like it?'

'I'm not sure,' said Rufus, 'how about you?'

'I'm already a full partner,' said Maro proudly. 'The old man's getting on a bit and lets me do more or less what I like. It's a great business, we're growing all the time and I've already made quite a pile of my own.'

'It's strange we haven't met before at market.'

'Oh, I hardly ever go to market myself, only enough to keep my hand in. That's the advantage of being the boss.'

'Well the life seems to suit you, Maro.'

'But you're not too happy with it, hey, Rufus? Well, each to his own taste. I tell you what, if you wait a moment I'll finish my business here and walk along with you.'

Maro returned to the men in the warehouse and spoke awhile to them. He seemed very much at home with his authority, handing out orders with great ease although the men were mostly twice his age.

Soon he returned to Rufus and they walked on together past the growling, fenced-in mastiffs. At first the conversation was mostly about the cloth trade. As they talked, Rufus noticed in Maro all those traits he was beginning to dislike in the trader's life: the cautious fishing for possible business or useful information, the valuing of everything in terms of the profit it returned, even the mannerisms and gestures he himself had started to use.

This at least is how it seemed to him though perhaps he was not being quite fair. It seemed to him that Maro was acting as a caricature of himself and his success in business only made it worse. Maro was not trying to boast, but his tales of various business coups made Rufus aware of how little he had yet achieved in life and the small prospect he had of doing so the way he was going.

'Is this what I'll have to become if I'm to get anywhere?' wondered Rufus.

After they had been talking in this way for a while, Maro asked him:

'Tell me, Rufus, what was it you were so busy thinking about when you nearly passed me back there?'

Feeling slightly embarrassed, Rufus explained about the table.

'Why, friend,' said Maro, 'if cash is your only problem, it's lucky you bumped into me. I can lend you whatever you need. How much is it worth spending on this thing, though? You say it's rather old and damaged as well. How about taking me to see it? It sounds as though you're not too sure about it yourself. Perhaps you need some cool-headed, impartial advice on the matter.'

Rufus then explained about the meeting at the coffee-house later.

'Well, that's fine,' said Maro. He thought for a moment, then went on: 'I tell you what, I was going to meet some friends nearby this evening. I'll see if I can round them up early. We can all meet at this place and pass judgement on your purchase. It promises to be an interesting evening, you may well see some more old faces you recognise today. You are an unfriendly fellow, you know, we've quite lost touch with you since the old days.

'Well, I have some more business to attend to this afternoon. I'll see you later, then, Rufus. I'll bring as many of the others as I can find. I shouldn't worry about getting the thing home; if you still want it we'll arrange something easily enough.'

They went their separate ways, Rufus walking along lost in thought again. The problem of transporting the table seemed to be solved, but Rufus wondered if it would be worth it at the price he'd have to pay. He was not particularly looking forward to this gathering of old friends, especially if they were all as settled and successful as Maro.

At the appointed time everyone gathered in the coffee-house gardens to await Grogul and his companions. Maro had brought six or seven others with him, two of whom Rufus knew from the old days. It was not such a strained gathering as he had feared. After a while Rufus relaxed and began to feel quite pleased with life. This certainly was a very strange day.

When the first coffee-pot had almost been drained, Grogul and his friends arrived with the table. The coffee-house was on the border between their district and the more respectable one to the south. Obviously they thought it a dangerous place because they were swathed in sacking up to the eyes.

They came up the road from the direction of the river in a disorderly huddle, bearing the table and its pile of oddments high on their shoulders, darting their eyes nervously about them. They stopped by the wall surrounding the coffee-house garden and peered over as if it were midnight and they were about to rob the place.

Grogul was the boldest and least disguised of them, but he seemed very put out when he saw the crowd that was with Rufus. He became as nervous as the rest. He turned to the others and whispered something, they promptly put the table down where they stood and scurried back down the road. Grogul, pausing only to call out, 'You know where to find us, sir,' followed suit.

Rufus jumped up and ran over to the wall. He had meant to pay them their silver crown then and there but he was too late. When he reached the wall and looked over, they had all disappeared around a bend in the road.

Rufus' friends had been much entertained by this spectacle. Some of them trooped out into the road and bore in the table triumphantly. They set it down on the grass, ordered more coffee and cakes, pulled up the chairs and everyone gathered round to inspect it.

All agreed that Rufus had a fine bargain. Clearly they also thought it was a rather eccentric one, but were perfectly good-natured about it. They reassured him that between them all, transport was no problem.

No-one said exactly how this was going to be done though. The conversation drifted away from the subject of the table onto more general topics, although some of them continued to rummage through the contents of the pile on the table.

At first Rufus was quite contented. After an hour or so, however, when his problem seemed to have been completely forgotten, he grew restless. He wanted to be off to pay Grogul and then go home. It would be quite a long ride in a cart. Also, the later they left it, the harder it would be to find one for hire. He was not self-confident enough to broach the subject again, however. He sat on in silence with the restlessness growing inside him.

The others' chatter then began to annoy him. He had never much liked simply sitting around talking and now, when he wanted to settle this business, it grated on his nerves. He didn't feel he could say anything though because he was depending on their goodwill.

This dependence was next to annoy him. He was annoyed with himself also for landing in this situation, a situation where he depended on the goodwill of others towards whom he did not feel much goodwill himself.

All in all Rufus gradually fell into a terrible mood. The last straw came when, trying to distract himself by looking for the jewelled cross he had particularly liked, he opened several of the little boxes only to find them empty.

'What a crowd of robbers you are!' he burst out loudly.

Dead silence fell upon them all. They looked at the little boxes lying open and empty, then at each other. One by one, sheepishly, they drew out the amethyst and crystal trinkets they had pocketed and returned them to the pile on the table. As it turned out, none of them had taken the particular cross Rufus had been looking for, it was still in one of the boxes.

'Didn't think you'd mind,' muttered someone. He did not finish the sentence, but Rufus felt he had implied 'since we're taking the rest home for you.'

As soon as he had opened his mouth, Rufus felt overcome with embarrassment, but of course there was no way of taking back his words. He tried to pass it off as a joke, saying there was only one particular one he wanted, that they were quite welcome to the rest, but his voice was not convincing enough. No-one took anything back from the table.

An awkward silence reigned. Rufus racked his brains for some way of restoring the situation but could think of nothing. In the end he said,

'Well, I suppose before we do anything else I'd better go and pay them. It's getting rather late.'

The young woman on his left said, rather tartly: 'I think, before you go off, that it's your turn to buy some coffee. After all, we are here to lend you a hand.'

'Of course,' said Rufus, 'I wasn't thinking.' There were no waitresses about so he rose and made for the building.

'Will you get some cakes as well?' called the young woman after him.

Rufus gave the order to the landlord. The coffee, cakes and sweetmeats were sent out quickly enough, but some confusion arose over the bill. First of all it was added wrong, then the landlord wondered if the right quantities had been listed on it, but of course it was too late by then to check because some of the cakes had been eaten. The landlord sat at his desk with a big frown, questioning the waitress who had taken out the goods and the one who had put them on the tray and so on. Rufus, of course, was growing more and more impatient. Through the open door he could see that evening was beginning to fall. He began to imagine that place down by the river in the dark with Grogul's friends lurking about. The thought was not at all comforting.

He then thought that perhaps Grogul would return while he was inside and take the table away, assuming he was not interested. The day was beginning to take on a mildly nightmarish quality.

He started towards the door to make certain of the table, but the landlord called out: 'Just a moment, sir, I think I almost have it.'

'Look,' said Rufus, desperately, 'I'm in a hurry. Could you not just charge me the highest figure you've worked out so far? That way we'll both be happy.' Apparently taken aback, the landlord did this and Rufus finally escaped by parting with just under half a silver piece.

It was a mean trick of the landlord's, but one which had often served him well. He could spot someone in a hurry in an instant.

Once outside Rufus excused himself to his friends, saying he had to leave before it was too dark. He walked hastily out of the garden and down the road towards the river. Once out of sight of the others he broke into a run.

He felt very stupid. 'How on earth,' he wondered, 'did I get myself into this ridiculous situation?' He wished he could have asked one or two of the others to go with him.

He had not run far when he heard his name called. He stopped and looked around. From the dark doorway of a ruined shop on his left came the voice again in a kind of loud whisper:

'Rufus, lad, come over here.'

'Who is it?' asked Rufus, pausing.

A figure drew forward out of the shadows. It was an old crone dressed in black, leaning heavily on a crooked, gnarled stick. Her face was turned towards him but her eyes weren't focused upon anything. There was a milky film over them. Rufus realised she was blind.

'I can't stop now, mother'—such was the way old women were addressed—'I have business to do before night falls.'

'I'd stop if I were you, Rufus.' Her voice was like the rustling of wind. 'You're heading for danger.' This statement being so much in agreement with his fears, Rufus retraced his steps towards her.

'How do you know this, mother, and how is it you know my name?'

'I am old, son. My eyes may be blind but I can see well enough without them.'

'What is it you see?'

'Do you know, child, there is one thing robbers hate above all else—that is being tricked and robbed themselves. I see, down by the river, a band of robbers who believe that is just what has happened to them. They've been stewing there for the last hour or two like the pot over their fire, believing themselves first of all made fools of and then robbed. If you go down there now, son, they'll give you little chance to offer your silver or explain yourself. You'll be lucky to escape with no more than a beating, Rufus.'

'What am I to do then, mother?'

'Go back, child, go back to the garden and wait for them there. They'll come, never fear, as soon as it is dark. They will not dare do anything so far from their lair and with others around. Put their minds at ease, say you forgot the time and were about to come to them. Pay them twice the sum you agreed upon and they will leave in peace.'

Rufus felt a wave of relief at finding some clarity at last amidst the confusion of this day. What she said made perfect sense. 'Thank you a thousand times, mother,' he said, taking her hand.

'There's something else, Rufus,' said the old woman.

'What's that, mother?'

'What made you behave as you did just now? You've not only offended your friends but have lost the help you needed.'

Rufus said nothing, only nodded. He was half-inclined to drop the whole matter, to pay Grogul as the woman had suggested and then simply to go home and forget the whole affair, leaving the table behind.

The crone lifted her walking stick and rapped Rufus sharply on the head with it. He jumped back.

'What was that for?' he cried, rubbing his head.

'For thinking foolishly, child; you've done enough of that today. Come back here and walk me along a short way.' Rufus gave her his arm and together they walked slowly back towards the coffee-house.

'Then tell me what I should do, mother,' said Rufus, 'and I promise to do what you say.' It seemed to him that she chuckled at this but he could not be sure. She said nothing for a minute or so as if to let his last words hang on the air. Despite the pain in his head from the knob of her stick, Rufus began to feel quite good-natured again. He had heard of people having second sight before but had never believed in it; he had certainly never expected to meet anyone who actually possessed it. He was so impressed by the old lady that he really was prepared to do whatever she told him. Strangely enough, it did not feel at all like a burden.

'That table,' began the old woman, 'is more valuable than you imagine. If you knew just how valuable you would never have fooled about as you have done today. However, it's a mercy you saw as much in it as you did and that you rescued it. Your job is not finished yet, but if you do just as I say, you should carry it off without coming to any harm. A little discomfort, perhaps, but no harm.'

'In what way is it so valuable?' asked Rufus.

The old woman seemed not to hear his question but continued as if he had not spoken: 'You've lost the help of your friends. At least, it would hardly be gracious of you to ask anything of them now, so what you must do is this: firstly, go back to your friends and return to them whatever they wanted before. Apologise for your selfishness and say you do not need their assistance after all. Say you have just made other arrangements. Secondly, you wait for your robbers to show themselves and handle them as I've already explained. Thirdly you give me whatever money you would have had left over.

'That should leave you in an interesting position, young Rufus. No money or friends to help you, just you and your table and a long way to travel. Mind, you must not leave it behind, you must promise me that, in return for saving you a deal of unpleasantness.'

'I'll promise, mother, but what am I to do, what can I do then?'

'Wait and see when the time comes, child. Now give me your hand and swear you'll do as I say.'

Rufus did so, though he felt she was being rather melodramatic.

'Good, good,' muttered the crone. Then she said sharply: 'If it means sleeping in the garden tonight on your table, will you still keep your word?'

'I will,' promised Rufus.

By this time they were approaching the garden wall of the coffee-house. The wall was on their right, the old woman pointed to the opposite side of the road, to a narrow passage between the buildings. Night was almost completely upon them now, the passage was pitch dark.

'I'm going that way, child. If you will be so kind as to cross the road with me, I shall leave you to your affairs.' They crossed the road. The old woman went a little way into the passage before turning to him. All Rufus could see of her was the lower part of her face and her hands. The rest of her melted into the shadows behind.

'Well, Rufus, give me your money now and go. Remember to do everything I told you.'

'I will, mother,' said Rufus, giving her the coins. 'Thank you again for your help. My half-crown and coppers seem poor payment for it.'

'Don't let it trouble you, child.'

She turned and instantly disappeared from sight as much as if she had vanished into thin air.

Before Rufus reached the garden he had enough time to wonder at his good fortune that such an old lady should have happened along. It was not pure good luck, however. Aznavor was not the only one keeping an eye on Rufus now.

What followed this strange encounter is best summed up quickly. Rufus went to his friends and did just as he had been told. He apologised for his rudeness earlier, said he had made other arrangements for moving the table and returned to them the trinkets which had taken their fancy. He said they could help themselves to whatever else they liked on the table before leaving, not even asking them to leave the particular cross he wanted for himself. Then he apologised again and so on.

The result of this repentance (which he overdid somewhat, not being used to such humility) was that Maro and the others saw completely through his act. They in turn apologised for helping themselves without asking and all were soon reconciled. Someone left immediately to find a suitable cart and everyone was much more enthusiastic about the venture than before.

In time Grogul and his companions arrived, were soon pacified and went away well pleased with their two silver pieces.

The table was loaded onto the cart and, after a long and pleasant journey across the city, which included several stops for wine and ale, Rufus found himself in the front hall of his house, pleasantly drunk, with his table, his amethyst cross and a pile of interesting junk.

—V—
The Old Woman in Black

When the old woman in black left Rufus by the coffee-house, she hurried off through the night with an extraordinary speed for one so old, let alone blind. She walked like a woman half her age. For a while she skirted round the desolate area by the river, following the darkest passages wherever possible. Then she turned away and headed south-east.

She passed through perhaps the roughest districts of the city, where crime and vice flourished like flies on a refuse tip; yet there was no trace of nervousness in her manner and she seemed to be in no danger. Cut-throats and harlots alike drew back politely to let her pass.

Meanwhile, at her destination, a meal was in preparation. Four people were gathered in a kitchen. A cooking fire blazed in the hearth and on the kitchen table was a pile of half-cut vegetables. Two of these people, a man and woman, were standing by the table deep in conversation. They had been cutting vegetables but their task was forgotten in the heat of the discussion. Their knives rested idly in their hands, or at most were waved in the air to illustrate a point. The vegetables were being treated similarly.

The other two, again a man and woman, were by the fire. The man, a small axe in his hand, was feeding the fire with freshly cut wood. The woman was putting a dish into a hollow in the hearth wall which served as an oven. The man, whose name was Cornelius, said with a grin to the woman beside him:

'It's a fine pair of spouses we have, Emra. If we weren't here to see things done they'd starve to death through talking so much.'

Emra smiled and they both watched the other two who went on talking, noticing nothing.

The man by the table was named Chrysol. He was tall and slim and had no hair. He seemed slightly older than the rest, being somewhere between thirty and forty years of age. The woman he was talking with was called Nuoma. She wore a long, blue, close-fitting dress and a sapphire ring. She seemed to be getting the best of the argument. In the faces of these two there was an expression of tension quite lacking in the two by the fire.

Each of the four seemed to have a special liking for a particular colour. With

Chrysol it was yellow; he wore a yellow silk shirt and boots of soft yellow leather. With Nuoma it was blue, Emra green and Cornelius red. There was an aristocratic air about them all, making them appear strangely out of place in that modest kitchen doing their own cooking. They did not seem to be aware or ill at ease about it, though.

Cornelius rose from the fire and went over to the other two. He put his arms around both their shoulders and gave them an affectionate squeeze. Startled, they stopped talking and turned to him almost with annoyance. Cornelius simply grinned back at them and after a few moments they all laughed and went back to what they had originally been doing. The tension in the air melted away.

The old woman had by now come to a pleasant district, passing through streets lined with cypresses and a few small public gardens where fountains played. She was not far now from where the four lived. The streets were quite well lit; she slowed her gait to that one would expect of the old, blind woman she was. She shuffled along, tapping walls and pavements with her stick, pausing every now and then to rest.

At last she came to the pleasant, smallish house which was her destination. She paused below the front door as if to gather her strength, then climbed the few steps up to it and hammered on the panels with the knob of her stick.

After a short while the door was opened by Chrysol. When he saw who it was he exclaimed with pleasure:

'Why, mother! It's good to see you. What are you doing abroad this time of the evening? Come in and be welcome, it's not often we have the pleasure of a visit from you.'

He gave her his arm and led her through the house to the kitchen at the back. The old woman changed her way of walking yet again. She appeared neither as feeble as a few minutes before in the street, or as Rufus had seen her, nor so strong as when she had hurried through the dark passages and alleys on the way. She seemed somewhere in between. She straightened her back and lifted her head, she walked not like an old crone but as a dignified old lady. Her hood fell back and her long silver hair glistened like the moon. Her face, though deeply lined, was firm and strong, her mouth calm and wise, her eyes like two large, glistening pearls.

The three in the kitchen were as pleased to see her as Chrysol had been. Cornelius pulled forward a chair with a cushion. Emra led her gently to it and, when she was seated, kissed her cheek warmly. She held the old woman's hand and knelt beside her on the floor saying: 'You're just in time to eat with us, dear mother.'

They treated her as if she really was their mother. This was not the case, though. The four called her 'mother' because although they had known her for years, the old lady had yet to tell them her real name.

'I have some news for you all,' said the old woman in black when the greetings were done. 'I have half a mind to keep it to myself for a while longer though.'

'News, mother?' said Chrysol. 'What news—good or bad?'

'Good news, son. I think it can wait, though. I think I shall wait until we're sitting down to eat before telling you. It can keep that long—and like wine, should taste the better for it.'

'Oh, mother,' said Emra in mock entreaty, 'how can you be so hard? How can you tell us you have good news then keep it to yourself?'

The old lady chuckled and stroked Emra's hair:

'Tell her, Cornelius, why I did it,' she said.

'So's your supper will be ready the sooner, mother,' Cornelius said, grinning. He went back to the fire and fed it with more logs. The others returned to what they had been doing, except Chrysol. At the old lady's request he pulled up a chair and sat quietly beside her, watching the others work.

The atmosphere in the kitchen was happy and busy, pleasantly spiced with expectation. No-one spoke much beyond a few comments on what they were doing. Cornelius went outside and could be heard chopping more wood in

the dark. A cool breeze came in through the open door, pleasantly stirring the heat from the fire and the cooking aroma.

At last all was ready and they sat down to eat, the old woman at one end of the table and the others at the sides.

'Will you tell us now, mother?' asked Emra.

'Patience, child. Should I tell you now and take your minds off this lovely food you've prepared?'

Nuoma took her cup and raised it in a silent toast to the old lady. The other three followed suit; clearly they realised she could see at least as well as anyone else despite the opaqueness of her eyes. Then they all set to work on the meal.

When all was eaten Emra said:

'Now, mother, we'll accept no more excuses; do tell us your news.'

'Well, children, I give in. The news is this, your table has been found.'

The four looked at each other for a moment as if they did not understand. Then Nuoma said: 'Our table, you mean *the* table?'

'Just so, child, *the* table, the one over which you took your oath.'

'Where is it, mother?' asked Cornelius. 'We must go at once and fetch it.'

'Now, Cornelius,' said the old woman, chidingly, 'if it was that simple, would I have kept you waiting this long? The table is safe enough, I have my eye on it. At the moment it's travelling slowly across town on the back of a donkey-cart, in the care of a young man who is on his way to becoming perfectly drunk for the first time in his life.' She chuckled at the alarm which showed in their faces.

'Don't fret,' she said, 'you can trust him to take care of it as well as getting drunk. He's sensible enough at heart.'

'Shame, mother,' said Emra. 'You're teasing us!'

'Who is this young man,' asked Chrysol, 'and how did he come by it?'

'It would take a while to tell you everything, dear,' said the old woman, 'but in short, this young man, Rufus, who at first sight seems to be quite an ordinary young man, is being drawn into strange affairs quite beyond his understanding. For this reason I have been taking an interest in him, partly to see if I can keep him from any great harm and partly to find out what's going on. It seemed to be pure accident that led him to the table, nothing connected either with you or the other business he's involved in, but one must never be too hasty in judging these affairs. Perhaps time will show both that he is connected with you and you with his other adventure.'

'Where was the table?'

'In a robbers' den down by the river.'

'How is it, mother,' asked Nuoma, 'that you never came across it before now? Can you not see anywhere?'

'This is a big city, child, and it's your table not mine. I've had no time to search the city for it foot by foot, and no lead to tell me where it could be. Before today I was not even sure it still existed. You have this young man to thank for its recovery. If he had not found it while I was watch-him, who knows when we would have come across it again, if at all?'

'But what use is it to us that it has been found,' asked Cornelius, 'if someone else now has it? If he saw enough in it to take it from the robbers, will he not want to keep it for himself?'

'You were ever impatient, Cornelius,' laughed the old lady. 'But put your mind at rest, I don't think you'll have to wait long, a week or two at most. That surely is not too much to ask, especially if it turns out in the end that he is related in some way to it and you. The table may have attracted him as it did Nuoma in the beginning. You see, the way he recovered it couldn't have been better if we'd arranged it ourselves. Rufus they saw only as an innocent youth out of whom they might make some silver. Such is their ignorance that they now think they've made a handsome profit, though all he gave them was two silver crowns. If you had stumbled across it as Rufus did, it would have been a very different story. Ignorance recognises its natural enemy. If they'd seen you I doubt if they'd have thought beyond attacking you for the sake of any valuables you might be carrying.'

'Have you any idea, mother, where it has been all these years?' asked Chrysol.

'I have a feeling,' came the reply, 'that most of this time it's been but a stone's throw from the robbers' den where Rufus found it, in an old temple beside the river.' She described the temple Rufus had seen. 'Though how it got there after being stolen from you and why it has remained there undisturbed all this time is still a mystery to me.'

'Come now, mother,' said Nuoma. 'I think you're teasing us again. We know that nothing can remain a mystery to you once you put your mind to it; why then do you talk to us of not knowing this and that as if you were any other mortal?'

The old lady smiled to herself and reflected a moment before replying. 'Well, child, let me put it like this: when I choose I can, as you know, see into the minds and lives of others easily enough, and I can go without fear of danger into places where others would be risking their lives, but this power I have only on the understanding that I do not pry or meddle beyond a certain natural limit. So perhaps in a way I could have found your table before now by working through you, and perhaps in the same way I could do many other things which may seem desirable, but in stepping beyond my limits I would lose the powers I use to do so.'

'But who is it that sets these limits and to whom are you held responsible?' persisted Nuoma.

'Why, I set them myself and am responsible only to myself,' laughed the old lady.

'But come now,' she continued. 'This is all beside the point. The point is that tonight your table has been found again and soon it will be returned to you. Let us trouble ourselves with no other questions. Let us drink to our good fortune and be grateful to young Rufus for what he has done.'

'Yes, we owe him much,' said Emra and the others agreed.

The talk went on for a while as the old woman in black filled in the details about Rufus and his finding of the table. Then, gradually, silence settled over them like a mantle. Silence broken only by the occasional crackling of the fire. They were all lost in thoughts of the past, of their involvement with each other and with the table.

Now, although there is much I do not know or understand myself, I shall try to relate something of the nature of the table and how it came into the hands of Chrysol, Emra, Nuoma and Cornelius.

Rufus had not been mistaken when he thought the designs on the table-top had something magical about them. The table did have such powers, that is how the four first found it.

As we have seen, most folk in the city did not believe in such things as magic. They thought such superstitions had been left far behind them, believing they had only ever existed in the fancies of the ignorant and the hoaxes of conjurors. Nevertheless, there were those in the city who practised magic and found it worked well enough despite the common opinions.

In their childhood Chrysol, Emra, Nuoma and Cornelius had believed in magic about as much and as little as any other children. Along with their friends at about the age of ten they had given up what belief they had and accepted the adult view of the world. It was only some time after the table entered their lives that they began to understand the hidden workings of nature.

It happened about the time Chrysol was fourteen, the others were between one and three years younger than him.

They all knew each other in those days without being particularly close. They were members of the same gang. They had climbed the roofs together and fought together against others, doing all that was usual for adolescents in that city. They had argued and flirted with each other, though no more than was usual and no more than with others in the same gang. Cornelius and Chrysol did not particularly like each other and often fought and quarrelled, Cornelius usually winning the fights and Chrysol the arguments. Likewise, Nuoma and Emra did not get along very well, Nuoma thinking Emra silly and Emra thinking her cold and heartless.

Still, as I have said, these feelings were no stronger than was usual and, being members of the same gang, they considered themselves friends.

It was Nuoma who started it all. She was always prone to wild impulses and one day a particularly strong one came to her: she wanted to go underground. This of course was almost unheard of. There was an unspoken fear, almost a dread of the cellars and tunnels over which the city was built.

The gang was lazing around, basking in the sun on the rooftops. Nuoma looked them over speculatively. When her eyes lit upon Cornelius she knew he had to come. She did not think of any reasons, she simply knew. Similarly with Chrysol, with whom she was quite friendly. Then, and much to her own surprise, she chose Emra. There was no-one else in the gang who seemed to fit although there were several with whom she was more friendly, particularly so than with Emra.

Nuoma was used to trusting her impulses. She gathered the three in a corner and told them of her plan. Of course, not wishing to seem cowardly, the two boys agreed, though each wished the other had not been invited. Emra surprised herself by agreeing also.

Nuoma led the way, not thinking at all about what she was doing but following her impulses in the way that pleased her most, leaving details like lanterns and candles for the others to take care of. When they reached the tunnels and deserted cellars she seemed in her true element, leading them to underground streams and even to great underground caverns in the bedrock of the city. The caves were damp and dripping. Stalactites and stalacmites reached patiently towards each other like rows of frosty teeth. The cave walls looked frosty also and were of all possible colours. Humps of rock loomed in the flickering candlelight like goblins silently watching them.

Being timid in those days, Emra did nothing very practical on the journey but simply followed the others. Her timidness, however, affected the others, heightening their own nervousness and making the journey feel all the more frightening and dangerous than it was already. Even Nuoma was slightly frightened, though she did not show it and not for a moment did she think of turning back.

Nuoma led on steadily as if she knew the way well. When the others urged her to slow down so they could keep track of where they were, she gently taunted them for being cowards and went on faster than before. It had not taken long after entering the place for the others to lose all sense of direction and become completely dependent on her. It's as well they did not know at the time that it was Nuoma's first trip underground as well or they would certainly have panicked.

Eventually Nuoma led them to an old cellar and there stopped. The cellar was piled high with interesting lumber. The doorway at the head of the steps leading to the building above had been walled up. The table was in the centre of the room, looking very much as it did when Rufus first saw it years later. Seeing the table, Nuoma realised that it was the point of the whole expedition. She called the others to come to it from where they were rummaging in the corners of the room. She sounded much older than she was; without thinking, they obeyed. Together they cleared the pile of old clothes off the table and dusted it clean. From under the black dust and cobwebs the table emerged fresh and clean, it was as bright a yellow as is possible for natural wood.

On the table's surface they found an inscription carved. After deciphering it, Nuoma seemed to realise what to do next. In the same strangely mature voice she told the others that they now had to take an oath. They were to swear by whatever they held most sacred that if any one of them knew of any of the other three being in need of help, they were to forsake all other ties and obligations to go to their assistance. This oath was to be binding for all time.

The boys were taken aback. They took oaths seriously enough never to have made any before. Even joining the gang had only involved a mild half-promise. Both were against the idea, particularly when they looked at each other and imagined what such an oath would involve.

It was Emra who spoke up in favour of the idea. The reason for it suddenly became clear to her and though she could not put the reason into words, she joined Nuoma in insisting the boys do it.

The atmosphere in the cellar, the strange journey which had led them there, the girls' insistence and no doubt, as they realised later, some influence of the table, all weighed upon the two boys. In the end they gave way and agreed.

Nuoma showed them what to do. Each stood on one side of the square table and joined hands with the others in a curious manner. The way in which they did so was this: with their left hand they held the upper forearm of the person on their left, between them they thus formed a square with their left arms. With their right hands they held the right hand of the person opposite, through the square. In this way each of them was touching all the others. Then they took their oath, repeating the words after Nuoma.

Afterwards they left, taking the table with them. This made the return journey rather difficult, but somehow they managed it.

The immediate effect of this alliance was great tension between the four. Their differences were so great that even Nuoma at times wondered what had prompted her to start the affair. Cornelius and Chrysol avoided each other much of the time, each hoping in that way not to know when the other needed backing up. Somehow, though, such situations always seemed to crop up whenever they did meet. In spite of all the difficulties they faced, however, no-one thought seriously of going back on their oath; they valued their honour too highly.

It was Emra who did most to smooth over the differences between them. This was because down in the cellar it may have been Nuoma who instinctively knew what to do, but it was Emra who instinctively understood the reason for it. Not for many years could she put this understanding into words. It was just a feeling, but it was a certain enough feeling to make her the diplomat of their alliance.

The next effect, which unfolded gradually as they persevered in their efforts, was that they found themselves to be the controlling force of their gang.

The third effect, which was excusable because they knew of no higher aim in life, was that their gang became the terror of the rooftops.

This is how the four came upon the table. After their gang broke up and left the roofs, they stayed together and continued to enjoy remarkable success in whatever they tackled, though it was not power they sought as they grew older.

It was several years before they overcame the problems raised by their conflicting natures. After four or five years they almost came to the point of going their separate ways altogether. The cause, not surprisingly, was love and jealousy. What took place and the way peace was brought about would make an interesting story in itself were there space to tell it. But the solution, with which they again surprised themselves, was that Nuoma and Cornelius married, as did Chrysol and Emra. After this the frictions between them gradually died away.

Not long after their alliance had begun to show signs of success, they began to wonder at the extent to which the table was responsible for it. Nuoma admitted she had no idea where the impulses had come from which guided her to it. The other three agreed that left to themselves they would never have thought of joining forces. So what was more likely than that the table itself had exerted some influence on them? The extent of this influence though and how much they continued to owe to the table, were impossible to judge.

The longer they stayed together and the more successes they enjoyed, so they treasured the table increasingly. But often they would wonder about the old question.

Later, when they came to know the old woman in black and discovered her wisdom, they asked her if she knew. Her first reply was:

'When we are born we forget our true natures. Much of our lives are spent simply uncovering that which was there all the time. This is the game of life, because it is only when we uncover that which was always there that true life begins. Sadly it is all too easy to miss our chances and not succeed at all. Sometimes we have to be pushed into being true to ourselves.'

When the four asked for a less cryptic answer she said:

'It's like this: if it were not for the table you may have missed your chance and would not be what you are today. But if you were not suited by nature to be what you are now, then no magic could make you so.'

At the time the four were not much wiser for the old woman's explanation, but later they grew to understand it better. One thing is certain: when they lost the table they no longer enjoyed quite the same good fortune they had grown used to. They had to work much harder for success. This often made them sad because it was usually for other people's good that they worked.

—VI—
Four Visitors

WHEN RUFUS arrived home with his table, his father had already gone to bed and was asleep. However, the noise of Rufus' friends downstairs woke him. He turned on his back and lay listening to the loud voices joking and singing, sounding very much the worse for alcohol.

'I knew he had taken to drinking,' thought the father gloomily. When the noise downstairs died away and the street door slammed, he turned on his side and tried to get back to sleep. It was some time before he succeeded. He could feel a hollow ball in his chest; it was hollow and full of cold fire. It had first appeared the other night when Rufus did not come home, it was then only the size of a marble but had been growing ever since.

The father did not know exactly what it was, it scared him. He knew it was no illness but beyond that he was doing his best not to see, for what also scared him was that if he did find out, there was not a soul in the world he could share the knowledge with. Too late did he realise that he and Rufus had never talked about anything but the passing incidents of the day, not for many years anyway. The only person he had ever really shared his thoughts with had been his wife, and she was long dead.

'Why' he wondered, 'has Rufus turned strange like this? Has he not had all he could ask for, and has he not been happy enough working beside me these years?' But even as he asked himself this, the father knew he had been too hopeful in supposing Rufus would simply grow up and take his place beside him without a trace of rebellion. Had he not added a few grey hairs to his own father's head?

Rufus meanwhile was not troubled by any worries or fears. He had been to the kitchen to pour himself a final jug of wine and was now sitting admiring the table by lantern-light. Around his neck hung the twinkling amethyst cross, strung on a silver chain, black with age, which he had found on the table. He sat on the stairs, leaning against the balustrade, sipping his wine and marvelling at how good life felt.

When his eyelids began to droop, he managed to drag himself upstairs to bed, kicking over his mug as he did so. The mug smashed on the floor, red wine trickled out across the flags of stone. The lantern burned on for a while till it ran out of oil and the flame guttered and reeked.

The following morning the father did not even bother to wake Rufus and ask him if he was coming to work. Downstairs he cleared away the remains of the broken mug and opened a window to let out the sharp, unpleasant smell of the guttered lantern. He examined the table curiously, wondering what on earth his son could want with such a dirty old thing. The assortment of curious objects, which were lying on the floor beside it in a sack, he found even more puzzling. The father prepared himself and set off for market alone.

When Rufus woke later and made his way downstairs, he found a note which had been pushed under the street door. The note read:

> 'Our new king will need a new bodyguard. If you are interested, be at the eastern gate before sunrise a week from today. The caravan leaves with the first light of dawn.'

The note was signed 'Aznavor' and bore the same curious mark beside the name which Rufus had seen before. This time he recognised it as a monogram, presumably of 'Aznavor' though in some foreign language.

Rufus spent the next few days working on the table, removing the dirt, stains and scorch-marks. This absorbed him so completely that he worked from first thing in the morning until far into the night with hardly a break. His father thought he had lost his mind, but left him to his own devices, hoping that whatever it was would burn itself out and Rufus would then return to his senses.

'Wait until he realises we have to work for our bread,' he thought with a certain grim satisfaction, remembering the days of his own rebellion.

As Rufus laboured, his first surprise was at the fresh yellow wood which soon emerged on the raised surfaces. His second was that what he had taken for vague spiral patterns within the circles in fact turned out to be inscriptions. In the large circle in the centre were several verses, then in each of the four smaller circles a couple of these were repeated. When he deciphered them the verses read:

round and round, down and up
each time you drink, you stretch your cup

if you wish the meaning of this rhyme to know,
round and round is the way to grow

round and round like the seasons' wheel
opens all doors to the past as well

round and round in a spiral way
gains the centre the quickest way.

Rufus could make no sense out of these verses, but he enjoyed the sound of them. Afterwards, as he worked, he repeated them over and over to himself and after a while the words themselves seemed to revolve round and round in his head like a wheel.

Something else he found as he scraped away was that, due to the different textures carved into the wood and the blackening it had undergone, the pattern emerged in pleasant shades of light and dark. This he improved upon by rubbing charcoal into the unburnt areas and treating them like the burnt ones. The pattern did not emerge quite as distinctly as in the drawing I have made of it, but the effect was much the same.

As he worked and bent his concentration on the practical task, the words of the verses revolved in the background of his mind and behind them lay the real problem he had to face, the decision about leaving the city to join a foreign king's bodyguard. No doubt it was because he could form no clear picture of its implications that he avoided facing it squarely. Apart from anything else, the walls of the city were also the limits of his imagination; even his wildest ambitions and daydreams had not ranged beyond them.

In a way it was obvious what he should do, considering the frustration and restlessness he had been feeling. But as is not unusual, Rufus found that it was one thing to be restless in the safety of a well-defined path and another to follow his convictions into the complete unknown. Like most people, what he wanted was the best of both worlds—a little adventure and spice together with an assurance that he would not be risking too much by it.

So, as I have said, this problem lay at the back of his mind and he put off facing up to it but it did not lie still. Like a flower the thing grew as if with a life of its own and out of the corner of his mind's eye Rufus could not help noticing its development.

He felt himself to be a spectator as his mind tentatively tried out the thought of leaving home. He watched as it ranged over all the people he knew, bidding them farewell. He watched as it ranged over the city, over familiar streets and places, over the small details of life which he had always taken for granted and which now became so precious. Strangely enough, one of his greatest pangs was at the thought of not seeing their donkey Ned again, not having him come up to have his ears scratched. Even though he was as a spectator to all this, Rufus felt a dull pain. He felt rather as a great tree must feel as its roots are dragged slowly but relentlessly out of the warm earth and the cold night wind whistles through them.

Rufus was discovering the contradictions of these dark mysteries, for at the same time as he felt like a tree being uprooted, he felt also that he was growing as light as a bird. At the same time he felt like a bird taking wing, he felt that the decision was growing within him like a flower. He felt it was not he who was making the decision but the decision that was making itself.

It's not surprising his father thought he was out of his mind, because that was very much the state he was in.

In those days Rufus hardly spoke to his father. He ate nothing but bread,

cheese and wine and only went out when he needed something for the table. He neither washed nor changed his clothes and only slept in his bed because the stone flags in the hall grew too cold in the middle of the night.

On the fourth day Rufus finished his work on the table and oiled it generously with sweet-smelling linseed oil. Then he cleaned up the hall and himself and changed his clothes.

He sat on the stairs and stared at the table as it drank in the oil and glistened like gold even in the dim light of that dusty place. The cross twinkled at his neck, the chain had been washed clean in his sweat and glowed softly. His father, returning from work that evening, was surprised to find him thus.

'What, son. Finished it, have you?'

Rufus nodded. Encouraged by this and by the improvement in Rufus' appearance, his father lit a couple more lamps and examined the table.

'Done a good job, son,' he said. 'It looked only fit for firewood when you brought it home the other night.'

As the father walked around the table he was also secretly examining his son. Rufus still had a faraway look in his eyes but they were not as completely vacant as before. His face was calm. The father grew more encouraged. 'Perhaps' he thought, 'the crisis is over.' His admiration of the job Rufus had done on the table was quite genuine but:

'What are you going to do with it?' he asked.

'What?' Rufus started.

'What are you going to do with the table? Are you going to sell it, or what?'

Rufus was puzzled and could not answer. It was a very good question, what was he going to do with it? The decision was almost fully grown in him, to be a foreign king's bodyguard, but it was still not his own decision. 'Why,' he wondered, 'have I spent all this time on it if I'm only going to leave it behind?' This question led to others and since so much had been happening inside him over which he seemed to have no control, Rufus was soon plunged into the greatest confusion. The calmness of his face disappeared, to be replaced by a burrowing frown and he stared fixedly at the floor as if the answer was to be found there.

His father noticed the effect his question had and decided to be more cautious, to give Rufus more time to recover. To change the subject he said:

'I'm going to make dinner, will you be joining me tonight?'

Rufus nodded and the father went off to the kitchen.

After dinner as they sat by the cooking fire with a jug of wine apiece, it seemed to the father that life might soon return to normal after all. The hollow inside him shrank a little. The only outward difference between that evening and many others they had passed together was that they both drank two or three times more wine than usual.

On the evening of the fifth day there came a knock on the street door. Rufus and his father had again been sitting by the fire with their wine. Rufus rose and went through to the front hall. On the doorstep, when he opened the door, stood four figures.

'Who is it?' called his father from the kitchen.

'I don't know,' called back Rufus.

The tallest of the four, who was Chrysol, stepped forward into the light and enquired: 'Master Rufus?'

'I'm he,' said Rufus.

'We've been told you have found something belonging to us,' said Chrysol. 'Or perhaps I should say something that used to belong to us.'

Rufus just stared at him rather blankly. Emra pushed forward into the light also.

'He means our table,' she said, 'a table you have found. The old lady in black told us you had it. Please will you let us see it?'

Still rather nonplussed, Rufus stepped aside and invited them in with a wave of his hand. When they saw the table, the faces of the four lit up with pleasure. They hurried over to it, seeming to forget all about Rufus who closed the door, then stood by it watching them with the faraway look in his eyes.

The four arranged themselves with one on each side of the table, looking down on it. Then in a murmuring, musing, dreamy kind of voice Nuoma whispered the words of the verse carved in front of her and each of the others followed suit. They did not do so in awe or seriousness as though it were some kind of religious rite, but more with the feeling one has when repeating a long-forgotten song and nostalgia washes over you. That is not quite how their voices sounded, but is the clearest I can describe it.

Rufus' father had come to see what was going on. He was standing in the doorway on the opposite side of the hall from Rufus, taken aback by the sight of the four by the table. They were certainly a fine sight with their silks and long, hooded velvet cloaks.

After several minutes during which everyone seemed frozen in these positions, the four seemed to come to their senses and realise where they were. Emra left the table and came over to Rufus.

'It's beautiful,' she said. 'I don't know how we can thank you for finding it.' She put her arms around Rufus and kissed him. The others followed and each thanked him in their own way. Nuoma, seeing Rufus retreat rather nervously as she approached him, took his hand and squeezed it. Her hand was as cool as fresh dew.

'Just a moment, though,' said Chrysol to the other three. 'I think perhaps we are being a little hasty. We're forgetting that Rufus knows nothing about us. He's probably had no idea anyone would be coming to claim the table on which he has been working so hard, whereas we have known about him for some days. Perhaps we should first introduce ourselves and then find out if he is willing to part with the table.'

All turned to Rufus who, after some hesitation, invited them through to the back of the house. His father was still in the doorway leading to the kitchen. Rather awed, he drew aside to let the four pass. As Rufus went by, however, he held him back by the arm.

'Where do they come from Rufus?'

'I've no idea, father.'

'Where did you get the table from then?'

'From some robbers down by the river.' And to avoid further questions Rufus pulled his arm free and hurried on after the four.

Over bread and bowls of hot soup the four introduced themselves to Rufus and his father. They seemed quite at ease, answering freely any questions that were asked. Naturally they said nothing about the true nature of the table. They knew they were with true city folk and would be misunderstood, but apart from this they were perfectly honest and open. While they talked, Rufus was only half-listening. He was preoccupied with thoughts of his own and it was the father who asked most of the questions.

Rufus was thinking about his decision. It seemed to him that now he had to choose either to accept it as his own, or reject it as a vain daydream. As we have seen, the decision up to now had seemed to have a life of its own, compelling him to go through the motions of taking his leave, but now was the moment of choice, the moment of free will.

It was in some way connected with what he decided to do with the table. If he gave it to these four he would at the same time be accepting that other decision. If he kept it he would at the same time be rejecting the open road. He would never then have the courage to leave the city, and from that moment on would gradually settle back into the life of a cloth merchant. As the old woman in black would have said, it was a fight between common sense and his own true nature with a dose of cold feet thrown in for measure.

The four seemed to sense something of the struggle taking place in him, for they let the conversation flow on without referring to or even hinting about the table. They talked mostly to the father.

In the middle of some completely unrelated story Rufus interrupted with: 'You're quite welcome to the table. I can see it means more to you than to me and anyway it clearly belongs to you.' With these words Rufus plucked the flower and claimed it as his own. Chrysol, Emra, Nuoma and Cornelius were delighted and thanked him as in the beginning.

'But what can we do for you in return?' asked Emra.

Rufus shrugged and said he needed nothing.

'You can be sure,' said Emra, 'that if ever we hear of a favour we can do you, we will do all we can to help.'

So it was settled and presently the four left with their table. Nuoma had said least to Rufus during their visit, but in leaving she had stopped beside him and touched the amethyst cross around his neck.

'Keep wearing this,' she said. 'It will bring you luck and make it easier for us to learn if you need help.' Then she joined the others outside and Rufus closed the door.

Now, Rufus' father was angry. The door was hardly shut before he turned on his son:

'Don't understand you any more, son. What put it in your head to do a thing like that? Those four were rich enough, it wouldn't have hurt them to pay you for the work and money you put into that table. It was enough that you should lock yourself away with the thing for a week and work like the devil on it, but then to give it away for nothing to rich strangers! It beats me! Can you explain to me why you act like this?'

Rufus looked at his father and the gulfs yawned between them. How could he begin to explain what he was thinking and how he had changed in the last two weeks?

The father could not have chosen a worse time to be angry. If Rufus had

had any lingering doubts, what his father had just said would have been enough to drive them away. Rufus shook his head and walked off.

The next night, when his father was asleep, Rufus packed a bag with whatever he thought might be useful, pocketed what savings he had, left a note for his father saying he was off to see the world and went out to the garden. As he went down the steep steps under which Ned slept, his eyes were full of the garden as it had been in the old days, before his mother had died. Under the waning moon the garden blossomed again as it had then, the white doves cooed and purred. He said goodbye to Ned with a lump in his throat and before long was running and leaping across the rooftops towards the east gate.

When he arrived there Rufus found a caravan assembling. It was the middle of the night, the city slept and the moon glimmered, but beside the eastern gate there was all the bustle and excitement of midday. Working by lanterns and the light from a few fires, the travellers made last-minute checks of their equipment and swapped tales and cheerful greetings with others. Camels and donkeys shuffled and snorted impatiently. A few women cried quietly at being left behind. Old women tended the fires over which coffee and soup stewed; they dispensed it freely to anyone wishing to keep out the chill.

Having come this far, Rufus now had no idea what to do next. He went to a fire and drank a cup of sticky black coffee while he surveyed the gathering. He quickly realised that compared with even the poorest of the travellers he was hopelessly ill-equipped for a journey. He had no thick robe or blanket to keep out the cold desert nights, he had even forgotten to bring his boots with him and had only the flimsy, slipper-like shoes he was wearing.

Rufus stood by the fire, sipping his drink and hoping that Aznavor had thought to provide a companion for his journey. He hoped also that the companion would be well-enough equipped to make up for Rufus. Luckily both these hopes were soon fulfilled. An amiable old merchant called Lazarus approached and introduced himself.

Lazarus had three loaded donkeys and had apparently been prepared for the worst, for he soon provided Rufus with all he needed. He chuckled all the while at the foolishness of young city-folk setting off into the world as though it were a stroll through a park.

With the first glimmer of dawn in the east, the city gates were opened. Amidst a din of shouting and farewells and dogs barking, the caravan filed out of the city and headed straight for the sun and the bleak desert.

—VII—
The City of Brown Gods

IT TOOK several weeks' travelling for the caravan to draw anywhere near its destination. After leaving Rufus' city and its waterfall, they journeyed for a long while over the flat desert plain. It was more steppe-land than desert, I suppose, since it was not quite barren, but to Rufus it was as desert-like as he could imagine. They followed a course slightly south of east, making for the mountains which rose over the horizon.

Rufus had never imagined the world to be so vast and empty. For days at a time they travelled with no sign in any direction of human habitation, no trees or streams or beasts, no hills or dales; just stones, dry earth, dry grass and thorny bushes. The villages and towns they passed through hardly seemed worthy of the name, often being no more than a huddle of a dozen or so small buildings amidst poor farmland. He began to understand why travellers were so unabashed by the patronising way in which they were often treated by proud city-folk.

After the plain they climbed into a jagged, wild, mountainous country. Upon reaching the highest pass they looked down over the diminishing mountains below to a second plain which lay beyond. This plain was interrupted here and there by huge brown rocks—small mountains even—which rose out of it. These were widely spaced, standing alone or in small clumps. Lazarus pointed out one of the largest of these and informed Rufus that that was where they were headed.

They descended the mountains without incident, losing sight as they did so of the mountain which Lazarus had pointed out, then set out across the second plain. The land was drier and more uneven than before. The road was barely perceptible, being no more than a track slightly more worn and less pot-holed than the ground beside it. In the baking summer heat the flies gathered round them in clouds. Invisible insects in the grass sang with a strange hard sound, making it seem that the earth itself was humming, or so it seemed to Rufus.

He and most of the other travellers walked the journey; the beasts were for carrying their goods and supplies. Once his blisters had healed and his feet had grown used to his boots and the rough ground, Rufus was happy enough.

He did not find the journey too strenuous since the caravan's pace was geared to the slowest of the travellers. Still, the constant exercise and the effects of sun and wind changed him in those weeks. He grew leaner and fitter than before, his face was soon well-tanned.

Lazarus had proved to be the best of travelling companions. He talked cheerily with Rufus much of the time and had begun to teach him the language of the city they were making for. It was his home town though he had left it while still young and had travelled most of the time since. Rufus was naturally curious to find out about the place and what he was letting himself in for, but Lazarus would not let himself be drawn beyond the most trivial details of life there.

'Have patience, lad,' he would say and cluck his tongue. 'Why be so curious when you know we're a secretive people? Save your questions for when we arrive, then you can ask all you like of this high lord who's sent for you.'

This of course did not satisfy Rufus. He tried questioning others in the party, but either they knew nothing or they answered him even more abruptly than Lazarus. In the evenings, after camp had been made and all except those on watch were sitting around the fires, talk and reminiscences flowed freely enough. But Rufus noticed that even then none of the folk from the City of Brown Gods talked of their home. Their tales would only be of adventures they had experienced on their travels elsewhere. In deference to them, it seemed, none of the others mentioned the place either, except in passing. So Rufus had to be content to wait.

'You must have some terrible secret to hide,' said Rufus good-naturedly one evening. Lazarus smiled but replied seriously enough:

'Perhaps, my friend, it's just that we have been betrayed too often in the past. Perhaps you're right and we are too secretive, but being too careful is often better than being too careless. In your city you've grown used to comfort and safety, and besides you think of nothing but yourselves. You can't imagine there is anything outside your city important enough to fear. Perhaps it's right for you to think so, I'm no judge, but for us it would be suicide. We're a small people and have many enemies. That may be our own fault, but even so we wish to be secure in our homes like anyone else. So we're secretive, it does no harm as far as I know.'

The mountain on which stood the City of Brown Gods rose again above the horizon ahead. Soon after this they made out something on the road a mile or two further on. Drawing closer, they came to a short square pillar on either side of the track, each surmounted by a stone statue. The statues were broken and worn by wind and sand. At first they looked strangely out of place, like a gateway without a wall, till they saw that beyond them the road changed remarkably. From being no more than a broken track it became a wide, smooth, almost undamaged road of sun-baked clay. As they stepped on to it, each traveller gave vent to a great sigh of relief. After what their feet had tramped over before, it was like walking on a carpet.

They gained this road during the second half of the morning. It was quite usual for them to halt for a while at noon, to recover their strength during the most scorching part of the day, but this day they carried on though the sun burnt as brilliantly as ever. The good road gave them strength and there were muttered wishes expressed of trying to reach shelter by nightfall. Indeed, the caravan's pace increased by almost half, the sweat poured in rivers down the bodies of men and beasts alike and there was little talking. The mountain continued to rise until it stood completely revealed. It rose like a jagged, sloping tooth from the plain, its sides climbing less and less steeply until they reached the topmost point in a gentle incline.

They kept to the new pace all afternoon, but as the sun sank below the horizon behind them and the mountain shadows overtook them, they did not seem to have come much closer to their goal. The caravan's leader left it until the last possible moment before he reluctantly called a halt. They drew aside from the road into a hollow and made camp. Donkeys, mules, camels and horses were unloaded and set to graze. Some of the travellers set up small tents, others simply took their sleeping gear and food to where the fires were being lit.

'The folly of people,' said Lazarus, shaking his head and smiling as he unloaded his three donkeys. 'It's always the same. When we come to the mud road we hurry on, hoping to make the city by evening, but we never do. We all know it would be a full day's march at twice our normal speed, but we try anyway. Still, we shall reach it early tomorrow, it's not as far away as it seems.'

There was a festive air in camp that night. Since there was no longer any need to ration their supplies, all did their best to finish off what was left of them. The fires, which were usually modest, were merry and blazing. The richer travellers freely shared the last of their food and drink with the less well-off and the conversation was on the whole as cheerful as at a feast. In one respect, however, they did not relax; the watch was doubled. As Lazarus said, there is nothing worse than being robbed within sight of safety.

Rufus and Lazarus sat together by a fire. Lazarus for once seemed rather melancholy. They stared into the flames together, watching the wood spit and flare, turning black, then red, then crumbling into the depths of the fire, glowing, crackling and slowly disintegrating. They sat in a little pool of silence amidst the general chattering. It was Lazarus who broke the silence.

'Well, it's the last night, Rufus,' he said. 'Tomorrow we reach the city and then our ways part.' He paused. 'So you're going to join the king's bodyguard, you say? Well I can't say I'd fancy it much myself, but there's no accounting for taste. If it's the world you want to see, there's no better way than being a travelling merchant. If it's adventure you want, we see our fair share of it. Not that we go out of our way to find it, mind you; there's enough around without any need for that. We've been lucky this trip, praise the heavens—

no bandits or lions or wolves. Let's hope nothing happens tonight to change it.' He was silent again for a while with an expression on his face which came as close to brooding as was possible for him. Rufus said nothing but waited for what his friend would say next.

'It's the lord Aznavor you're going to see is it?' said Lazarus. 'Well, he's a rum one he is. How you fell in with him I can't imagine. I don't want to know either,' he went on quickly. 'No more than what you've told me already. Myself, I always keep clear of powerful men; always will do if I can help it. It's a two-edged sword power is, and there's not many with more of it than lord Aznavor in our land. Still, I daresay there's folk that know how to handle it and it's not up to me to question the doings of our lords. Here,' he said, coming to himself with slight alarm, 'I've been going on as if you were one of us!' Then he relaxed again. 'Ah, well, I'm sure there's no harm done, not if you're joining the king's bodyguard. You'll no doubt find out all there is to know before long.'

They talked on for a while longer about other matters before taking themselves to bed.

So eager was the party to be moving the next morning that they rose and began to load their animals before dawn, fumbling around in the dark to do so. Before the sun came up they were on the road.

The road curved so that they approached the mountain almost from the north. As the sun climbed into the heavens it lit the eastern half of the mountain, revealing the city which spread down from the great building at its peak. Though warned that it was smaller than his own, Rufus was disappointed when he realised how small an area this city covered. Still, by any other standards it was a fair size for those times. The mountain was a harsh-looking place, rough and bare with deep fissures running down its flanks and sharp pinnacles of rock standing out everywhere like towers. Often it was hard to distinguish the rocks themselves from the city's buildings.

In a few hours they reached the foot of the mountain. One moment the road was flat and straight, the next it was winding and climbing steeply through one of the fissures. Most of the time, from then on, there were steep walls on either side of the road. In some places the way had been hacked through the rock or cut into a cliff-face, but for the most part it followed natural channels. They soon came to some more brown statues set either in the rock walls or perched on outcrops. These were fierce and warlike, some threatened to topple boulders down onto the path, others held swords and spears and scowled ferociously down at those below.

'Those are the Guardians,' explained Lazarus. 'Some say that when enemies try creeping up to the city unnoticed they sound an alarm in the High Temple. Whether or not it's true I can't say. Others say that at night they can do more than just raise an alarm; that they can move and fight of their own accord, but again I know nothing about it. I do know that the bodies of strangers are sometimes found on the mountainside cruelly cut to pieces. No-one claims any knowledge of the deed beyond saying it is the work of the brown gods. It may be that these are just stories put about to keep away our enemies or it may truly be the work of the gods, I don't know. The old gods are not as powerful as they once were, but perhaps they are still strong enough to defend us in this way. But either way it works well enough, we have few intruders.'

'I don't understand,' said Rufus, 'how such a peaceful, reasonable man like yourself can worship such wild and strange gods.'

'I wouldn't call them that too loudly when we reach the city,' warned Lazarus gently. 'But anyway, my friend, how can you hope to judge such matters when you yourself have no god at all? You see they may seem wild to you, and even to some of us at times, but the ruler of them all is the Smiling One.' Then Lazarus realised again he was talking too freely. 'Ah, Master Rufus,' he said, 'here I am doing it again, talking before thinking. But look ahead now, we're almost there.'

By this time they were about halfway up the mountain and the road was beginning to climb less steeply. A short way ahead it passed through a gate piercing a high wall. The wall stretched away out of sight around the mountain on either hand. It was not completely man-made; in places it blended into unclimbable cliffs or sharp rock pinnacles.

'This is but the first wall,' said Lazarus. 'There are two more, they circle the mountain completely. We call them the Three Crowns of the Smiling One. The main city lies within the inner wall and right at the top stands the Citadel and High Temple.'

After a brief delay while their credentials and goods were checked, they were allowed to pass.

Between the first and second walls lay farmland. So Lazarus called it, anyway, though stranger farms would be hard to imagine. The ground was as rough and convoluted as below, but in every hollow, nook and cranny, and on every ledge no matter how small, grew crops of all kinds. Sheep grazed in tiny meadows, fruit trees grew in the most precarious places. It was all well-organised, however. A network of paths and steps interlaced all these patches of greenery and channels cut through the rock carried water to each plot.

'You admire it?' asked Lazarus. 'This place was almost barren when my people first came here. Over the centuries we have carried the earth up from the wilderness below and brought the water down from above and so, through the kindness of the elements, this mountain became our fortress, home, farm and temple.'

There were a few scattered buildings among the farms, some clinging to the mountainside, others hollowed out of it. There were also more statues than below and of a less fierce nature.

Between the second and inner walls the land was much the same except there were more and larger buildings. Also some of the pockets of earth had been cultivated purely as gardens.

Passing through the inner wall, after a third brief examination, they arrived in the city proper. It was almost too much for Rufus to take in at once. The streets wound through the city like passages in a maze. On all sides buildings and natural stone towered above them. Where a pile of rock was a suitable size it had been hollowed out and its sides pierced with windows, or else it was partly hollowed and partly built onto. Rufus would find himself beside what he thought was a building, only to look up and find it was the lower part of a cliff which had been carved out. Everywhere he looked, the mountain and city blended in a most confusing manner.

To add to his confusion there were multitudes of statues. Wherever he looked he found grinning, laughing, weeping, grotesque statues staring at him. They sprouted in almost every possible place like trees in a fertile valley. There were also some statues of the plump, smiling god and he realised then that they had not passed any of these on the lower slopes of the mountain. There were fewer of these statues of the chief god than of the others, but on the whole they were larger.

The streets were crowded with rather wild-looking folk, wilder than Rufus was accustomed to, anyway. Many carried arms quite openly and wore light armour, women as well as men. Of the rest, most wore at least a dagger at their waist.

'It's not always as crowded as this, my friend,' explained Lazarus. 'Our people have gathered from far-off places for the crowning next week. By now most who are able to come will have arrived; there will only be a few late-comers like ourselves still trickling in. We like to celebrate these events in a fitting manner, you see, and a king is not crowned every day.'

'What became of your old king?' asked Rufus. It was a question he had asked more than once before without success, but he was hoping that in his present mood Lazarus might explain the matter. He was not in luck, however. Lazarus merely shrugged and smiled enigmatically.

Most of Rufus' travelling companions were to lodge at the same inn. They arrived at the place not long after noon. Rufus stayed long enough to bathe, change his clothes and have something to eat. Then, outside in the street with his bag over his shoulder, he said goodbye to Lazarus.

'Well, farewell then, young Rufus,' said Lazarus. 'I can't say I'm happy to see you go; taken quite a liking to you on this journey I have and that's saying something. I've never taken to partners before, I like to choose when to be alone and when to join in with the company, you see more of where you're going that way. You make a fair companion though and no doubt you'd prove your worth in a scrape. If you don't join the guard after all, remember you're welcome to join me on the road. You'll see more of life with me than by standing to attention half the time at some gate in the Citadel. Not that I'm

tempting you, mind; the lord Aznavor must have taken a fancy to you and if the likes of him thought I was meddling in their plans they'd have the hide off my back. Still, if you don't get the job you'll find me here for the next couple of weeks. If you want to get in touch with me after that you can leave a message with the inn-keeper here. I'm sure to be back sooner or later. Take care of yourself then. I must say you look more of a man now than you did a few weeks ago. We must have worked the puppy-fat off you, or the city-fat more likely.' He laughed and slapped Rufus in a friendly way on the shoulder. Then he explained how to get to the Citadel and Rufus set off.

It was easy enough to find even in that maze-like place: you simply kept walking uphill. Rufus came to a large gate in a high wall, beyond which towered the building. The Citadel was an awesome building of huge proportions. Except for one distant part, which Rufus assumed to be the High Temple itself, the place was not as lavishly adorned with brown statues as that other, far off Temple of Brown Gods, nor even as much as in the rest of the city below. The strength of the building lay in its sheer size and the massiveness of its ancient stones.

Impressed though he was by this sight, Rufus was not overwhelmed. On either side of the gate stood a sentry. Other guards could be seen in the courtyard beyond. Bearing in mind why he was there, Rufus sized them up, comparing their strength with his own. He was pleased to find that, taking away their arms and their black leather and steel armour, he felt himself to be a match for any of them.

The prospect of becoming a soldier and possibly having to fight did not trouble Rufus unduly at that moment. He was certainly not a violent person, but he had been used to fighting as a youngster and more recently he had at times had to visit parts of his city where robberies and knifings were quite common. More than once he had defended himself against such attacks without coming to any harm, so no doubt it was in these terms that he thought about a soldier's life. Perhaps he would have thought twice about it if he had realised just how peaceful his own city was compared with others in those times.

Rufus presented himself to the guards and asked to see Aznavor. He handed them the last note he had received together with one given him in parting by Lazarus. The sentries inspected the notes and passed him on to those by the guardhouse within the gates. They inspected the notes and one of them led him fifty yards or so to a small gate and handed him over to the sentries there. They in turn inspected the notes and passed him on to some more not far away. And in this way Rufus progressed through the Citadel with his notes becoming grubbier and grubbier until they were almost illegible. The changes in his escort did become less frequent, however, the further they went in.

Finally he was escorted into an enormous courtyard in the heart of the Citadel. By this time the afternoon was well advanced and much of the courtyard was in shadow. On the opposite side, in the northern wall, there rose a gigantic arch reaching almost to the height of the buildings. Within the arch, as in the Temple of Brown Gods, sat a giant statue of the plump, smiling brown god, sitting cross-legged like a cobbler. This statue was even larger than the other. Its face and half its body were in shadow, the rest of him stood out in sharp relief against the gloom behind. As they crossed the courtyard towards the arch, Rufus made out six or seven galleries running round its inner walls. The rest of the walls were alive with the smaller brown gods.

They passed through a low opening just to the right of the great arch. After stumbling up a short flight of stone steps, which he could hardly see in the sudden darkness, Rufus found himself on the lowest of the galleries. On his left ran a waist-high balustrade between the pillars, beyond it loomed the enormous statue's foot. It was almost golden in the afternoon sun; the largest toe was about the size of a man's chest.

The gallery stretched away ahead of them. Several doors opened off it and midway between each door was a niche in which stood a small statue. Besides these statues the gallery was quite bare of decoration. A short way on, the guard turned to the right through an open doorway beyond which rose a stairway. Up this they climbed to the topmost gallery, catching a glimpse at each level of different portions of the smiling god's body.

The highest gallery was more or less the same as the first except that from up there they looked down onto the top of the giant statue's head. At the far end, just beyond the point where the passage turned the corner, stood two more sentries flanking a wooden door. Rufus' escort showed them the remains of his notes and the two of them were permitted to pass.

'Enter!' called Aznavor's rasping voice in reply to their knock. Rufus' guard opened the door and followed him a few paces into the room.

Aznavor's chamber was pleasant and airy. Being on the north side of the building it escaped the sun and was refreshingly cool. The far wall was completely lined with windows forming a large bay, part of which was taken up with a raised platform covered with rugs and cushions. In the other part stood Aznavor, leaning against a window-frame and looking down on the mountain and city below, ignoring for the moment his visitor.

He was wearing the same green and yellow robe Rufus had seen on him before. Looking beyond the man and out of the window, Rufus caught his breath. For the first time since he had arrived in the city could he see beyond its rocks and stones. From that room he could see completely across the plain to the far-off mountains in the north and west. Far away through a gap in the mountains glimmered a lake or sea. The mountains themselves wavered in the heat still rising from the plain.

Aznavor turned.

'Well, well,' he said. 'Master Rufus! You're here at last. I watched a caravan arriving from the west this morning and wondered if it could be yours. I must commend you on your promptness. I didn't expect to see you till the morning.' He smiled through his rotten teeth. Rufus had forgotten how unpleasant that smile was and how wolf-like his eyes were. For a moment he wondered what on earth he was doing so far from home, having come on the word of a man he had disliked at first sight. The feeling passed, though; Rufus attributed his previous dislike of the man to that part of himself which had been a trader. After all, Aznavor could not help being ugly. Also, he had proved true to his word so far and Rufus owed his escape from the trader's life to him. Yet somehow he could not quite bring himself to feel for Aznavor the respect owing to a powerful lord. He was perhaps more on his guard against giving offence than before, but that was as far as it went.

Aznavor dismissed the guard and invited Rufus to sit with him on the cushioned platform looking out over the plain.

'Well, Master Rufus, this is certainly very different from our last meeting. So you want to be our king's bodyguard, do you? A wise choice, if I may say so. I found the trader's life rather tiresome myself. It's as one of his personal guard that I have you in mind; the man you're to replace has a weakness for secret plots which are a nuisance to keep track of. It would be pleasant for a change to have someone who is both honest and trustworthy, who won't be tempted to meddle in state affairs or pilfer from the treasury. A bodyguard's job is to protect the king and the king's job is to rule the people, don't you agree?'

Rufus nodded and then asked: 'Excuse me, I don't wish to seem ungrateful but there's a matter which has been puzzling me and that is, why have you picked me to take this man's place? I have nothing to do with your people and until I met you I didn't even know they existed. I've heard that in my city you don't usually even allow foreigners into your temple, so why is it that I was allowed in and why invite me here to be one of your king's guard?'

'Well,' replied Aznavor, after a pause, 'your question is understandable enough; the answer is quite simple, though. You are no foreigner, not enough to matter anyway. You may have been born in a foreign land, but it's our blood that flows in your veins. Your mother was completely of our race and even your father is partly so. When I first happened to notice you my first thought was that you were one of us. Only after that did it occur to me, for reasons I've already explained, that you were also perfectly suited for the guard. Were you never told about your mother's family?'

Rufus shook his head. 'Beyond my father I know of no other relations,' he said, 'and he never discussed matters like that. There's something else I've been wondering about, though, if you don't mind my asking. It's this: when we met, you were pretending to be a trader whereas here you're clearly a very important man. Now surely that wasn't all on my account, just to find out if I was likely to make a good soldier?'

Aznavor laughed. 'I'm sure I won't be disappointed in you, Rufus; you have a clear eye and don't suffer from vanity. You're quite right, it was for a completely different reason. Finding you was quite incidental. That's not to say it wasn't a very fortunate encounter. I could see right away how useful we could be to each other. This matter of replacing the old guard has been at the back of my mind for some time, but I was waiting until I found someone suitable before taking any steps. Apart from his dishonesty the man has the manners of a pig, so when I saw you I thought, besides the other good reasons, what could be better than to replace him with a civilised young merchant thirsting for change and adventure? But let's return to business. You guessed, of course, that there is a contest involved in your replacing him?'

'Contest?' asked Rufus rather suspiciously. 'What kind of contest?'

'You hadn't guessed?' asked Aznavor in surprise. 'I thought you'd realise. Still, I suppose I should have known better. Don't worry about it, there's no danger involved; your worst risk is a few bruises but I'm sure it won't even come to that. Take heart, you have nothing to fear and everything to gain. Let me explain:

'The situation is this: the customary way of removing one of the personal guard from his post is to prove he's no longer competent to hold it. This is done first of all by one of us denouncing him as incompetent, then he's bound by honour to invite anyone who thinks himself better than he to come forward and challenge him in combat. Naturally the weapons used are not real ones, they're dummies with blades of either lead or wood; it would never do to have the cream of our soldiers hacking each other to pieces. That's the contest, then. If the result is not completely obvious, we have a council of judges to settle the matter. So the defendant either stands or falls by the strength of his arm, the will of the Smiling One and the perception of the council.'

Rufus interrupted uneasily saying: 'But what makes you think I can match, as you say, one of the cream of your soldiers? I've never handled weapons before in my life.'

'I said don't worry, Rufus. Do you think I'd have brought you all this way if I was not quite sure of you? In the first place this man has grown fat, lazy and corrupt since he was any good as a soldier. He's held on to his post more through cunning than anything else. When challenged in the past he's quietly disposed of the challengers before the contest, pretending they ran away at the last moment in fear. So successful was he at doing this that he's not been challenged for years. He's played his tricks long enough, though. This time we've made sure he can do nothing. Unfortunately you're not the only challenger, but more of that in a moment.

'So, you need have no doubts about your safety and certainly none about your strength. As to skill with weapons, I've arranged for you to have the best possible instruction in the nine days left before the contest. That will be more than enough time for you to learn what you need to know. Though he's practising like a demon at the moment, the old guard has no chance of working off his fat in that time. He only learned of the contest a week ago!' Aznavor burst out laughing in his strange rasping way.

'As for the other contestants,' he continued after a while, 'who I imagine have been put forward by other lords, I was a little worried for a while that one of them might beat you to the prize. But having inspected them, I see now that there's no great danger on that account. You see, when there's more than one challenger the defendant has to face each in turn but he chooses the order in which he does so himself. Now, out of the five in this case you look the freshest from the cradle by far, if you don't mind my saying so. Being both stupid and a bully, our champion is sure to choose you first, hoping to make such an example of you that the others will lose their nerve. It will be a fitting end to his term of office. When you've beaten him (and I think that in his case the judges will allow you to go a little further than usual), the contest will be over. The other four will have to accept the result for two years at least, that being the time which must pass before you in turn can be challenged. And so justice will be done and everyone will be satisfied. Well, almost everyone, anyway.'

'It seems a little unfair on the man who's being challenged,' said Rufus, 'to have to face each of us in succession.'

Aznavor shrugged. 'The system has always worked well enough in the past. The defender can rest as long as he likes between bouts and if he so wishes, he can ask the judges to postpone the rest of the contests for a day or two. Also, there's one thing you forget, having been brought up in your city. Here in such a contest it's not only the strength of those taking part which counts, but also the will of the Smiling One who ensures that no great injustice takes place.

'Anyway I shouldn't worry about the fairness of this particular contest. If you knew half the evil this man has committed you would consider such a trial too lenient by far; if he wasn't so stubborn he could always retire gracefully without a contest. However, if it still seems unfair to you after you've won, well, you can always resign and leave. No-one will try to stop you. No doubt the four who had no chance to prove themselves would be highly delighted. It's true that I'd be disappointed in you, but I wouldn't force you to stay against your will. So, is there anything else troubling you? Do you want to change your mind now you know what your coming here involves?'

Rufus thought for a while but could not come up with any real objections to the scheme. Having come so far it would be foolish to back out now merely at the prospect of a few possible bruises. As to the fairness of the contest and whether or not he really wanted to stay in this place, there would be time enough to think about that later. As Aznavor said, he had nothing to lose. If he won the contest he still had a free choice. If by some chance he lost he could always join Lazarus on the road. The thought of joining Lazarus was actually quite tempting, anyway, but having just abandoned the trader's life, it seemed pointless to fall straight back into it again, even if it was a rather different kind of trading.

After thinking for a while along these lines, Rufus told Aznavor he was satisfied.

'A wise decision is always better for having been made twice,' said Aznavor. 'Well, if that is all, I shall have someone show you to your quarters.' He rose and ushered Rufus towards the door. 'I'm afraid you'll not have much freedom in the next nine days. Your training will take up most of your time, anyway, but also for your own safety it would be best not to leave your quarters. The guards you'll have there have been hand-picked and there's no chance of any treachery, but if you should wander about anywhere else in the Citadel I'm afraid we can't guarantee your safety. Still, it won't be for long; after the contest you'll be as safe as any of us so I trust you'll not find your confinement too unpleasant. The contest is on the day before the king is to be crowned. If all goes well, you'll be able to join his bodyguard for the ceremony.'

Rufus was led off to his quarters.

—VIII—
The Contest

RUFUS' QUARTERS were pleasant and clean, though rather spartan. They consisted of two rooms on the first floor of one of the Citadel's out-buildings. The window in the larger room looked down onto a small bare courtyard with a wooden post standing in the centre. The yard was bordered on the far side by the high Citadel wall. The room itself contained a large plain bed covered with bleached woollen blankets, a table, a couple of chairs and three doors. One opened onto a narrow stair leading down to the courtyard, one communicated with the rest of the building and was continually guarded, presumably as part of the safety measures Aznavor had mentioned. The third door led to the smaller room which contained a bath for use after the day's training. The bath was unusually efficient, having both a drain and a supply of hot water.

It seemed that these two rooms and the courtyard below were all Rufus was to see of the city for the next nine days. His meals were brought to him there and his training took place in the yard.

His trainer was a grizzled old soldier called Shasta. He had a gruff manner and rarely spoke more than was necessary for his teaching; even then he communicated mostly with grunts and gestures. He demonstrated the use of various weapons to begin with and then concentrated mainly on the handling of the short sword and dagger which were to be used in the contest.

There were two sets of these instruments. One was the dummy sword and wooden dagger which Shasta used when displaying the actual tricks of combat, the other was a pair of real, steel-bladed weapons with which Rufus was encouraged to attack the wooden post in the yard. The post was soon reduced to splinters and had to be replaced several times in the nine days.

Rufus soon found that the lead sword was not quite as harmless a weapon as it had sounded. The blade had a core of iron or steel which was only coated with lead. It was certainly blunt enough and there was little danger of losing any limbs by it, but clearly it could still be used to inflict considerable injury. So he practised hard and conscientiously, bearing in mind that it was easy enough for Aznavor to be confident when he would only be watching the contest.

For the most part he was quite happy to be confined to his quarters. In the evenings he was too tired anyway to do more than lie on his bed gazing up at the progress of the moon and stars through his window. On the fourth or fifth day, however, his curiosity did get the better of him.

On the morning of that day an unusually noisy procession passed by on the other side of the courtyard wall. In that place they could hear very little of the goings-on in the city and the sound of the procession reminded Rufus that the festivities leading up to the forthcoming coronation must by now have reached quite a high pitch. When Shasta left at midday for lunch, therefore, Rufus decided to forgo his own and take a look at what was going on outside. He shinned up the wall easily and dropped to the ground on the other side.

After a short walk through quiet back streets he came to a more crowded part of the city. Despite the noon heat the streets were full of people either wandering aimlessly like himself or going from place to place in processions. Rufus wandered along trying to make sense out of the noisy, colourful, teeming, chanting, praying confusion until his attention was caught by a knot of people clustering excitedly together by a rough stone wall. Curious, Rufus joined them and elbowed his way to the front to see what it was they were so worked up about.

In the wall there was a rough niche and in this lay the source of the excitement. The niche had been empty but now a sticky brown liquid was oozing from the stone at the point of its arch and collecting in a pile on its base, growing like a strange treacly stalagmite. The crowd watched open-mouthed in amazement. At first Rufus did not understand their awe but then he realised that the oozing mound was settling itself into a definite shape. Then he gaped too as he realised that before his eyes there was forming a perfect statue of the smiling god. Within a minute of the statue being completed, the liquid had set and become as solid as the wall itself. Indeed it looked just as if it had been carved from the same stone.

The crowd burst out with cries of wonder. Some knelt and prayed, others danced around singing praises to the Smiling One who allowed them to witness such miracles.

Rufus returned to his quarters very puzzled. Fortunately he found his way without much difficulty. He climbed back over the wall and dropped into the courtyard to find his instructor just returning from his meal. In his pidjin version of their language Rufus questioned him about what he had seen. The surly old soldier just said gruffly: 'It didn't used to happen as often as it does now and I bet there are a fair number of stonecutters around who would be happier with less miracles.' Then he put Rufus to work again.

After what seemed much longer than nine days, the morning of the contest finally dawned. Rufus awoke to knocking at his door. He rose and drew back the bolts to find Aznavor himself there with his tray of breakfast. In addition to the usual items there was a little glass of amber cordial. Aznavor entered and placed the tray on the table. He stayed and talked for a minute or so, apparently making sure Rufus was still self-confident enough, then he wished him good luck and made for the door. In the doorway he turned and said:

'Oh, by the way, Master Rufus, don't forget to take that cordial. It won't give you anything you haven't already, but it will bring out the best of what you do have, if you follow me. Even the best of us have to guard against making fools of ourselves at times,' and with that he left.

As it happened. Rufus was feeling slightly queasy at that moment and not on his best form at all. He wished now that he had seen his opponent and at least had some definite idea of what to expect. Looking out of the window he noticed some clouds in the sky. It promised to be a cooler, fresher day than usual and he did not feel much in the mood for fighting. Just then he wished he had never heard of the City of Brown Gods. Listlessly he drew on his armour of black leather and steel, and buckled on the belt bearing the sword on one side and dagger on the other.

After a light breakfast however, he felt much better. Whether it was the effect of the amber liquid or merely that he was now properly awake, he did not trouble himself to question, but simply felt grateful for the calmness and strength. It now seemed as good a day as any for meting out punishment on a bully and gaining honour as a soldier. An unusual sentiment prompted him to draw out the amethyst cross which still hung by its silver chain at his neck. He gazed at it for a while, then kissed it before returning it to its place. He left his rooms and set off with an escort through the Citadel.

He was taken to what was clearly a very old part of the building. There were few statues here and the walls were of roughly dressed stone, bare and uneven. The passage floors were worn an inch or two deeper in the centre than at the sides, though from the freshly disturbed dust it was clear that these corridors were seldom used. There were no windows and the walls were slightly damp, making him feel that their way was leading them into the mountain itself. The oil lamps burning on widely spaced ledges cast a dim, shadowy light; their footsteps echoed hollowly away before them. At length Rufus was shown into a room where four others waited and was left with them.

The four were dressed similarly to himself and Rufus supposed them to be the other contestants. No-one said anything, though a couple of them nodded noncommittally in his direction. Rufus sized them up and found, as Aznavor had said, that he was by far the mildest-looking of them. The others were either more bristled or scarred or bolder of face, but they were no larger and probably no stronger than him. They in turn were sizing him up and presumably also wondering about the likely order of the contest and the chances of being beaten to the prize. Still, Rufus felt no hostility in the air as he joined them.

The room was small and bare like the corridors outside. To the right of the door, in the adjacent wall, there was an open arch leading to the next room. The partition between the two rooms was only solid for the first three feet or so from the floor, above that was a finely carved stone screen. Through the screen drifted the muted sound of voices, for in the next room were gathered a number of important-looking folk holding conference. Soon Rufus made out Aznavor's figure amongst them.

The door opened and a sixth warrior entered the room. He stood just inside the doorway, holding the door-handle and surveying the five. None of them needed to be told that this was the man they were challenging, though to Rufus at least he was nothing at all like his description.

The man was slim and dark, his armour was something like theirs though not quite the same. His hair was long and black, held back from his face by a leather thong around his head. His face was lean and handsome, finely

featured and with its muscles tensed, betraying not the slightest flicker of emotion. His grey eyes ran over the five with cool calculation. His arms were lean and bare apart from a couple of leather bands: they were tensed, as was every other muscle in him. He looked as hard as iron.

A spasm of panic shot through Rufus. Where was the flabby old bodyguard who had held his place only by cunning and deceit, who had been slaving for the last couple of weeks to work off his fat and the effects of corruption?

This man was anything but flabby, and whatever else he was, he certainly did not look corrupt.

The dark warrior completed his inspection, closed the door quietly behind him and strode through to the other room where he joined the conference. Horrible suspicions loomed in Rufus' mind. He looked at the other four; they too seemed uneasy. Then on impulse Rufus drew his sword a little way from its sheath. The steel blade glinted like silver, the edge was as sharp as a razor, no thick blade looking like a flattened lead pipe. The sense of betrayal was complete, Rufus felt as though he was drowning in it. There was no time to think or plan. The assembly in the other room was filing out through another door. Aznavor appeared in the open arch for a moment and grinned evilly.

'Did I tell you,' he drawled, 'that the rules do not permit anyone to withdraw on the day of the contest?' Then with a whirl of his cloak he turned and left. Several guards entered to escort them to the contest.

They were led some distance to a great hall. The walls were lined with tables, leaving a clear space between them on the sand-strewn floor as the arena. The tables were loaded with food and behind them on benches sat a boisterous crowd of spectators eating and drinking with gusto despite the early hour. A hush fell over them as the five entered and they left off their meal. The challengers were led to a small open room on one side. There they found the champion making last-minute adjustments to his armour. He pulled on a black leather mask which hid the lower part of his face, making him even more inscrutable. The panic in Rufus spread as he struggled not to let it show. Again he felt he was sinking. All strength seemed to drain from his limbs, his arms hung like putty from his shoulders and his legs grew numb.

Deliberately, the dark man approached the five. His grey eyes slowly scrutinised them again. Then, with jabs of his finger, he pointed them out in the order in which he was to fight them. To his indescribable relief Rufus was chosen to go last. Why this was so he could not even begin to guess, but along with the relief a little warmth returned to his limbs and he regained at least some power over them. The champion turned away to a grinding-wheel in the corner of the room and whetted his sword-blade with a screech that rang chillingly through the now silent hall. When it was honed to his satisfaction he turned and gestured unceremoniously with it for the first contestant to precede him out onto the floor.

It was a mere few minutes before the first challenger fell deeply wounded to the ground. The champion jerked up the challenger's head by the hair and with one blow severed it from his shoulders. Then he held up the dripping, slack-mouthed thing and displayed it to the cheering, stamping audience; lingering finally with it held out towards Rufus and the others. Then he tossed it contemptuously to one side where it bounced out of sight under a table and returned to the little room. He brushed past the remaining four and sat in a chair facing the wall with his feet up on a stool. He laid his bloody sword on a mat beside him on the floor and casually picked a bunch of grapes from a nearby bowl. Lowering his mask he coolly ate the grapes while his breathing slowed to normal. Outside in the hall the cheering fell to a buzz of discussion.

After what must have seemed an infinitely short space of time to the next in line, the defending champion rose again. He went to the corner and honed his blade as before without troubling to wipe it clean first. Flecks of blood speckled the wall red behind the grinding-wheel. Then with the same casual gesture he signalled his next victim to precede him into the arena.

The second fight seemed set to last longer since this contender had more self-control than the first. He was restraining himself from making a scared and clumsy attack like the one which had led the first to his end. The champion himself made no attack, he was taunting the other with his superior skill, inflicting small wounds here and there with the point of his sword and cutting the laces which held together the challenger's armour. While this was going on, Rufus was distracted by some movement away to his right. Turning, he found Aznavor attracting his attention with small movements of his hand. How such slight motions could have caught his attention Rufus had no idea, but then Aznavor waggled his fingers again and somehow Rufus understood him to be saying that the champion was scared.

Not surprisingly, Rufus wanted nothing to do with Aznavor and certainly was not prepared to trust anything he said. He turned back to watch the fight, but somehow his whole point of view had been changed. He now saw that this time Aznavor had told the truth. It was only small things that convinced him, but they all added up to the fact that the champion really was scared. 'But why is he scared?' wondered Rufus. 'Surely not simply of us challengers; we're not in his class at all.' Whatever the reason, though, the man certainly was scared. All he had done up to now appeared to Rufus to have been an act to hide this fear, to scare his opponents into losing all hope. Even his present tactics now seemed to betray a lack of confidence in himself. He did not dare attack but was counting on his opponent's lack of nerve to give him victory.

When the second dripping head was held up to the spectators and then towards the little room, Rufus looked past it into the champion's grey eyes. There he found the final proof he needed; he saw fear and not only fear but disgust with this butchery. When the champion found Rufus' eyes on his own, he flung away the head in the same contemptuous manner as before and resumed his seat. As he sat there eating grapes as before, an awful suspicion grew on Rufus. He felt that all of them fighting that day were the victims of some dark plot of Aznavor's, the champion as much as his challengers. For a while he almost pitied the dark man as much as he pitied himself, but not for long.

Whether or not the champion too had been deceived into this fight, he seemed determined to keep his own head on his shoulders at all costs. As the next two contenders went the same way as the first, a stronger feeling than pity grew in Rufus, it was Self-Preservation.

As the moment for his own turn approached it happened, as it sometimes does in such situations, that his strength returned. His panic and fear ebbed away and his mind became as sharp as a needle. All he had learned in preparation for this day came back to him as he weighed up his opponent with a calculating eye. He still had to admit that the champion was more than a match for him physically so his only chance lay in trickery, in turning the champion's own tactics against him and playing on his fear. Such are the straws we clutch at when desperate.

Perhaps what followed is best described in the words of one of the spectators as he recounted it to a friend later:

'Well, there was four heads down see and he was back in the little room again, then comes the grinding again as he gets an edge on his blade. It was a good trick that, you could see it rattle them. They were all chickens, anyway, they looked pretty rattled to start with. When they came in we wondered what put it into their heads to think they could match him. Still, as I was saying, there were four down and one left. A youngster he was, foreign-looking. When his sword's done, the youngster comes out before him like all the others and that's when it started. We weren't expecting much, not after the other four and this one looking as rattled as the rest. But now out he struts cool as a cucumber. He stops by the table and turns to Gamil and says something in his ear, soft-like so no-one else could hear. Whatever it was it shook Gamil, I can tell you, you could see him turn pale. Then the youngster comes on and they start fighting, cautious-like, neither taking any chances. Then the youngster steps back and throws down his sword with a clatter and says he don't need anything so big for the job. He pulls out his knife and tells Gamil to keep his sword because he'll need it. Well, you could see he didn't know what to do, he stood there with the sword in his hand and the youngster prancing about in front of him like a cockerel, waving his knife. Then he took a step forward, still with the sword in his hand and the youngster leaps on him and sinks the knife in his throat! In no time it's all over and Gamil's dead, though not before he whispered something to the lad.

'Well, it took a while for us to take in what had happened, I can tell you. There was a dead hush in the place. The youngster too when it was done, he didn't prance around any more. For a bit he just stood there with the dead one hanging round his neck, then he pushes the body away and just stands there looking down on it like he didn't know where he was or what had happened. Didn't take the head from its shoulders like he ought to, didn't do anything but stand there dazed-like.

'Then we all come round and raise a mighty cheer but still he stands there. We climb over the tables and someone tells him to take the head, but he won't move. So the lord Aznavor does it for him and holds it up in the youngster's hand for all to see, though if you ask me he did more of the holding than the youngster. Anyway, then we carry him on our shoulders to the High Chair and we all cheer the new king. But he only gets more confused and keeps looking round saying "Where's the king? Where's the king?" Then of course we'd all forgotten his name not expecting ever to hear it again, so old Aznavor calls for silence. Well, he whispers in the youngster's ear for a while, then he turns and tells us his name. So with a roar that nearly lifts the roof we all sing out "Hail, King Rufus!" Though if you ask me we've got a bit of a rum king this time.'

—IX—

The New King

IT MAY not seem an unpleasant thing to be tricked into winning a kingdom but Rufus was overcome with repugnance. The horror of the fight and the knowledge of the death at his hands stayed with him throughout the next few days. In a daze he went through all the ceremonies of crowning, the celebrations, processions and feasts. He walked, sat, waved and even smiled to order. He wore rich robes and sat on a carved brown throne to be crowned king, he was cheered wildly by the people of the city, he sat in the highest place in the citadel surrounded by priests murmuring incantations and all this passed before his eyes like a vague and misty dream. From the moment he rose in the morning until he went to bed at night Aznavor was at his side controlling him like a puppet. Aznavor himself was highly delighted with Rufus' behaviour; it exceeded his highest hopes.

The only time Rufus came to himself at all was when he saw a statue of the plump, smiling god, and then it was only to shudder. As he was paraded around the city he had many occasions for such moments because statues of the Smiling One were oozing from the stones at an unprecedented rate. People said He was displaying his approval of the new king.

When Rufus shuddered at these moments, some words Aznavor had spoken before the contest rose afresh in his memory. The words were these: 'There's one thing you forget having been brought up in your city. Here in such a contest it's not only the strength of those taking part which counts, but also the will of the Smiling One who ensures that no great injustice takes place.'

What really happened in the contest was not quite as it appeared to the spectators. Certainly Rufus had put on a good show of bravery, and his taunting of the champion for his fear had quite an effect on the man, but these tricks had not in themselves been enough to tilt the balance so dramatically in his own favour.

Rufus' act had been one of sheer desperation. When he threw down his sword and leapt on the king, he did so because he knew he couldn't keep up the pretence a minute longer. When he actually leapt, two unexpected things happened. The king, shaken though he was, did have a fair chance of sinking his sword into Rufus' undefended stomach, but as he swung his arm to do so, some invisible force seemed to freeze him as still as a statue. Besides this, when Rufus found himself at the other's neck, he could not bring himself to deliver the fatal stab, but again some invisible hand drove his knife sideways into the king's throat.

How the dying man managed to say anything coherent at all after such a wound was a miracle, but what he did say was: 'You poor fool, do you envy a slave so much that you must kill him to steal his fetters?'

Having felt the way the invisible force had put victory into his own scarcely deserving hands, Rufus naturally remembered what he had been told about the Smiling One tilting the scales of justice when necessary. This is why he shuddered whenever he saw a statue of Him. He remembered all the butchery, and the blood which had gushed into the front of his own armour and thought: 'What kind of justice is this? How can that smiling, serene face hide such barbarity?'

It speaks for both his disorientation and honesty that Rufus did not try to explain away what had happened and attribute his success completely to his own skill and cunning.

After a few days, though exactly how many he was not sure, Rufus was left mercifully in peace. The main part of the ceremonies had come to an end and when Rufus had begged to be left alone, Aznavor had agreed and said he would arrange it. So for a while Rufus was left alone most of the time in the king's apartments, only having to attend a few special feasts and celebrations in his honour.

The king's apartments were spacious and luxurious, consisting of several rooms, a balcony facing the west and a private staircase leading to a paved area on the roof of the building. This area could not easily be reached in any other way and it was here that Rufus spent most of his time, sitting in a little stone pagoda and staring at the distant mountains. There were few parts of the Citadel higher than this place and Rufus had an almost uninterrupted view of the horizon.

These apartments were in the same mass of building as Aznavor's. In fact one of the smaller doors opened onto the same gallery, the seventh, in the arch which housed the giant statue of the Smiling One. It was a door which Rufus avoided using, but Aznavor frequently came that way when he visited his new king.

They had a strange relationship, Aznavor and Rufus. After the contest Rufus had felt nothing but loathing for him. He had only done whatever Aznavor said that day because he was incapable of thinking for himself. In the evening, when Aznavor first took him to the king's apartments, Rufus had roused himself with the departure of the guards and turned angrily on him hissing 'Liar and traitor!' His hand was on the hilt of his sword and such was his pain and confusion that he thought of turning it on Aznavor. The memory of the king's widow attacking him with a silver dagger was still fresh in his mind. He had not defended himself, but others had stepped in and saved him. The guards had dragged her away kicking and struggling, tearing her crimson dress in her efforts to break free.

Aznavor, however, was quite unafraid of Rufus' anger. He did retreat a few steps but did not seem alarmed.

'Calm yourself, Master Rufus,' he said, 'or perhaps I should say King Rufus. You call me a traitor for plucking you from a mean and thankless life and making you king? I really am sorry for having to spin a few tales in order to do so, but I assure you it wouldn't have succeeded without them. Before you do anything rash listen to my reasons; if when you've heard them you still think me a traitor, then do with me what you will. You're the king now after all and I'm but a lord.' Rufus did calm himself, or at least stood his ground.

'Not all I said was untrue,' continued Aznavor. 'In fact, if I remember correctly, there were only three points on which I changed the true story. The first was that the contest was only to be for a place in the king's guard, the second was that the contest was to be with false weapons and the third was that the man you were to fight was fat and degenerate. Shall I explain the reasons for these three untruths? Well, the reason for the first was that I knew you'd not believe me if I invited you here to be king. I knew my judgement was sound, but one of the qualities I saw in you was modesty and your modesty wouldn't have permitted you to imagine such a thing. The reason for the second was that I knew you wouldn't agree to an armed contest because it would seem too barbaric for you, which is exactly why we need a man like you for king. We're still a barbaric people by many standards, it's time we became more peaceful. At least it's time we put aside unnecessary violence, but to do this we need a peaceful king. In the past our kings had no desire for such changes at all. After all, they owed their own success to their skill as warriors and, of course, the pride of warriors is such that they never expect to grow old or weak or lose the favour of the Smiling One.

'As to the third falsehood, I told you he was fat and degenerate because we needed you at the height of your fitness for the contest. Worry wouldn't have helped you there at all. Again, it was not completely untrue; he may not have been fat but his mind was primitive and brutal. We're much better off without him.

'So these are my lies and the reasons for them. Don't you agree that they've been justified by the end? We now have a civilised young king and can begin to change our ways. The changes will be accepted because it was seen that you won your place in a fair contest.'

'But it wasn't fair!' burst out Rufus. 'I didn't deserve to win and anyway I don't want to be king!'

'Not fair?' asked Aznavor, surprised.

'Not fair at all,' repeated Rufus and he explained what really took place.

'But if what you say is true,' said Aznavor when he had finished, 'it changes nothing. On the contrary it proves that justice was done. Surely you realised it was the hand of the Smiling One at work? As to your not wishing to be king, that is surely the best of reasons for being one. It's wanting to be king that destroys so many of them.'

The chief effect of this conversation was to prolong Rufus' complete bewilderment for several days, making him once again incapable of deciding anything for himself. He still truly hated Aznavor for involving him in this scheme with its bloodshed, but whether Aznavor or his plan were evil in themselves he could not fathom out at all. Rufus felt overwhelmed by his ignorance. Was this kind of thing quite normal in the world and was his own home so unusual because this would never happen there? Were these people evil in applauding the disposal of the kings in this way or was Rufus himself just naïve?

As far as trust went, there was really very little choice in the matter. Whether he trusted him or not, Rufus had to rely on Aznavor. He was always by his side in public and was the only one who both knew what was going on and to whom Rufus could turn.

If he could have made up his mind either way about Aznavor, much of Rufus' confusion would have disappeared. He was almost prepared to believe and accept Aznavor for this reason alone, but he couldn't forget the evil in the man's face when, just before the contest, he had told them it was too late to back out. Nor did the dying king's last words seem to fit the story. He also felt there were other lies Aznavor had told him, but his mind was not clear enough to remember them. So although he continued to do whatever Aznavor said, Rufus was not at all happy about it and he wasted much fruitless energy over the question of right and wrong.

In the midst of this confusion and sense of isolation, Rufus finally remembered Lazarus. He almost kicked himself for not having thought of him before. Why had he thought Aznavor the only person to turn to when he had a true friend here in the city? Rufus immediately despatched one of his guard to enquire after Lazarus at the travellers' inn where they had parted, then he paced his apartments in restless trepidation. Would Lazarus still be there? It must be well over two weeks since they parted and that was as long as he had expected to be staying. Also, and worse if it were true, had Lazarus been a party to the deception, had he known all along the real reason for Rufus' being brought here, making a pretence of friendliness on the way? And were the guard really loyal to him or were they controlled by Aznavor, would his message ever reach the inn?

Fortunately for Rufus none of his fears were justified. When Lazarus had seen him as the king going in procession through the city, he had been almost as startled as Rufus himself. His first thought was to leave the city as soon as possible, but some instinct held him there restlessly against his will. He had been hoping for nothing to come of it, but was not therefore surprised when a soldier came looking for him and told him the king wished to speak with him.

Rufus' heart leapt when the knock came at his door and Lazarus was shown in. He ran forward crying: 'Lazarus dear friend, you don't know how glad

I am to see you!' Lazarus however drew away from him. Seeing this, Rufus stopped in the middle of the floor and dismissed the guard before approaching him again. Lazarus still backed away awkwardly and Rufus hesitated.

'Why, Lazarus, why do you back away? Can't you see you're my last hope? Say something, won't you?'

'Well,' said Lazarus cautiously, 'it's hard to know what to say when you're not sure who you're talking to. Are you the young runaway who travelled here beside me or are you the king? If you're the king, how am I to know how to address you, must I speak from my knees and call you lord, or what? For I've no idea how it's done, being nothing but a humble traveller. And if you're the young Rufus I knew, how can it be that you're now the king?'

Rufus was greatly relieved by these words and said: 'Come, Lazarus, sit down and I'll tell you all that's happened since I last saw you. Then you can judge for yourself who I am.' So saying, he sat down himself and proceeded to relate the story.

When he had finished, Lazarus stared thoughtfully at the floor for a while before looking up and smiling. He rose, came over and shook Rufus' hand.

'Well, now I understand clearly enough, young Rufus, though if I'd heard the tale from other lips I may not have believed it. Who would have thought there were such goings-on? You must have wondered what part I played in it, eh? Well, fool that I am, I was well chosen for the job of bringing you here. I knew nothing about all this, of course, but I couldn't have kept you in the dark better if I'd tried. And it was I who said that no harm came of being secretive.' He shook his head and smiled remorsefully. 'I can't begin to apologise, lad, I can see how unhappy you are. I see also that if I'd answered more of your questions this may not have happened. Still, we can't undo the past, we can only build on it. If I can help you in any way now I'll do my best.'

'Stay with me, then,' said Rufus. 'You're a wise man and have seen the world. Stay with me, you could understand what goes on here where I would be lost.'

Lazarus was silent and looked down sadly. At last he said: 'It pains me, young friend, that your first request of me should be one I cannot fulfil. No, wait. Say nothing till I've explained. I'll stay if you insist but it would do you no good if I did. You see, power and responsibility is the one thing I've always avoided, that's why I travel and never stay long in one place. It's easy for me to do so and I don't fear the perils of the road as many do. What I do fear is power and if I stayed with you what would I be but a king's adviser, a lord? You say I'm wise, but it's easy to be wise when you've not put yourself to the real test. If I were truly wise and not just wise enough to know my own weakness, why then I'd stay as you ask without hesitation, especially since I'm partly to blame for your unhappiness,' he paused.

'What I fear about power is the way it changes people and how few can resist it. I know for certain that if I stayed it would change me, and not for the better. I only hope you can bear it better than I. Beware though, already it's affecting you. You speak differently now and it's not just your misery that makes you do so. If I were to stay and were able to remain as I am, are you sure that in a while my manner will not begin to seem rough and disrespectful? After all, you're the king and the highest lords will be bowing to you. You look up to me now as an older friend who's seen the world, but will this still be possible when you grow accustomed to being king and looked up to yourself?

'No, wait. I'm talking nonsense. Take no notice of what I've just said. I'm trying to excuse myself and really only saying what would happen to me if I were in your place. Perhaps you're not like me at all and pride is not your weakness. What I say of myself is true though. If I stayed my head would be sure to swell before long, then I'd be worse than useless to you. If this was the first time such an offer had come my way, perhaps I'd take the chance, but it happened before when I was not much older than you. It wasn't a case of becoming a lord or anything so grand, but at the time it seemed important enough to me. Perhaps one day I can tell you the story, but for the moment let it be enough to say that I took the chance then. My head and heart swelled like pumpkins and I became as proud as a peacock. Then times went bad, my pride was shattered and I took to the road again. I failed the test, you see, I ran just when I should have stayed and pieced my life together again without making the same mistakes. I understood it all later, but my pride never did, it was only injured and never grew up. I know it still hides somewhere inside me, thirsting for revenge and wanting to parade itself again, but it's too late now for me to do anything about it.

'Believe me when I say this. Don't tempt me again and ask me to stay because I'll do so and then you'll find out what an unpleasant man I once was.'

These words made Rufus sad but he accepted them.

'Well, Lazarus, I'll not ask you again though I still feel less able than you to cope with this mess. It's enough that I'm in it and you mustn't blame yourself at all for my position, you were tricked as much as I. Tell me though, do you think Aznavor's to be trusted?'

'That's a hard one to judge, Rufus. From what you tell me it seems possible that his reasons for tricking you were as he said, though it makes him a misguided man at the very least. He thinks the end justifies the means, but from what I've seen of life the means aren't that easily dismissed. They have a habit of cropping up again when the end seems to have been won. To me that's the best of reasons for not being too devious or dishonest though the lord Aznavor seems not to care.

'I should be careful if I were you, for his tricks may well run deeper than he admits to. What you must do before deciding is to find out where his heart lies. If it's as he says and it's the good of our people he has at heart, then he's merely a misguided man to use such deception. You could trust him well enough though, as long as you kept your own hands clean and also had the good of our people at heart. Then if his tricks all backfire, the chances are they'll only land on his own head. If his trickery goes deeper and it's only his own interests he has at heart, then he's not to be trusted at all.

'Since I was last here it seems he's made himself one of the highest lords in the land. Now he's put himself at your right hand and you know nothing about the country of which you're the king, it's clear he's become the most powerful man of our people, at least for the moment. That's why you must make certain of his heart before trusting him, be on your guard! He's always seemed a good enough lord in the past, but what do the common folk know of politics in the Citadel?'

'I almost feel tempted to ask you to stay again,' said Rufus gloomily. 'What hope have I here in this wild place? Tell me though, Lazarus, how is it that if you knew nothing of this plan you still talked of the crowning of a new king? Surely you couldn't have known it would be a new king until after the contest. What if he'd won?'

'Ah, Rufus, it was a cunning web you fell into, that's just our custom. You see, when the king's called upon to renew the people's faith in him, he waits for the right season and then steps down from the throne. It's as though he'd died. He continues to live here in the Citadel, but from then until the contest he's no longer called king. He no longer rules or appears to the people, the lords rule in his place. Then if he wins the contest, he's crowned as our new king even though he ruled before. It may seem strange to you but that's the way it is. When the people or lords lose faith in him he dies and in the summer is born again, whether it be the same man or not, such is our custom.'

'And is it the custom also for the contest to actually be a battle to the death?'

'I'm afraid so. It's harsh I know, but those taking part usually know the stakes and their choice is a free one. There was talk some years ago of changing the custom but it seems now to have been forgotten. At the time it was said that the Smiling One himself pronounced such a change to be on the way, but no more came of it. Though we must seem a cruel people to you, Rufus, don't judge us too quickly. As I told you before, we're a small people and have many enemies, so we've needed a warrior king to lead us into battle. Though the contest may be harsh, its purpose is both to ensure that the king has the faith of the people and that deposed rulers aren't added to the list of our enemies. I believe myself that the time for such contests has passed. We've no real need to go to war any more and should instead be making peace with our old enemies, but apparently that time has not quite arrived yet.

'When I was young and set off on my travels, my head was full of thoughts very much like yours must be now. I was sick of our violence and the ease with which some of us take up arms and slay each other. Yet over the years as I travelled, I found it was not so easy to cut myself off from the past. I grew to love my city again in spite of its rough ways. As I said before, they aren't quite as they seem at first. Besides, I found that people elsewhere were much the same. Even in a city like yours life is not so very different, though perhaps the cruelty is better hidden.

'Also, my people are changing. Since the Smiling One came to us we've been losing our wild ways. Though as a youth the change seemed to me too slow, now I'm not so impatient, perhaps it will last longer for having grown slowly. Now I understand how some of our customs are changing I don't mind them so much. Now I know how imperfect I am, I no longer mind that my people won't be perfect in my lifetime. And though I may not like the way in which our king is chosen, I still came to see him crowned and rejoice with the rest of my people. No doubt this custom too will pass away as the Smiling One carries out his plan.

'Since you know nothing about our religion, Rufus, let me give you your first lesson. You see, before the Smiling One came we were ruled by the brown gods. As you've said, they're a wild-looking lot and truly they were wild, so were we in those days, much more so than now. We fought as wildly amongst ourselves and with other races as the gods did amongst themselves and with us. They were wild and ruthless and perhaps some of us would have preferred peace, but they were gods and we were only men. We couldn't say, as you would, that they were too harsh for us so we'd have no more to do with them. They were our gods and they ruled us with rods of iron. It was as simple as that, there was no choice in the matter. They still ruled us when we first came and settled on this mountain, and their rule wasn't as bad as you might imagine since much of what you've seen here was built in those days. Then, quite recently as the histories of nations go, the Smiling One came.

'He wasn't a god, yet he conquered all our wild and unruly gods. I won't say what we believe him to be because you probably wouldn't understand yet, but anyway, he wasn't a god, yet he conquered the gods. He didn't do this with force but with compassion. Force they understood only too well but compassion they couldn't understand at all so they fell to it one by one. Being compassionate, he didn't try to destroy them but under his rule they changed, just as we as a people are changing. At times both we and they forget him and return to our old ways, but never for long because he's the lord of us all.'

'But if this is true,' interrupted Rufus, 'and he really is so compassionate, how could he take part in such a bloody affair as the contest, how could he have made me kill your last king?' Rufus explained again how the fight had ended.

'Now that,' said Lazarus with a puzzled frown, 'is something I can't make out either. I can understand Him leaving the contest as it is because we're not yet ready for a change, but that He should actually take part in it as you describe is beyond me. It sounds more like the work of one of the brown gods, but how could He have allowed such a thing to happen? It must be that for some reason it was the only way to prevent your death. Or perhaps lord Aznavor is right and the Smiling One wants a peaceful ruler, though it seems strange to me that this is the only way it could be done.'

'Well,' said Rufus gloomily, 'I see I have much to learn if I'm not to go the same way as the last king. Do you think there's any way I can abdicate?'

'I've no idea,' replied Lazarus, also in a gloomy tone. 'I've never heard of it being done but perhaps there is a way.'

Depression spread its dark mantle over them and they sat for a while without talking. Then Lazarus sat up. He cocked his head as though listening to something, though there was no sound in the air. His face brightened and he stood up.

'Come Rufus, we're being too gloomy by far. Such misery has yet to solve anything by itself, and what great worries are there to trouble you so much? You're in no danger for the moment, it's two years at least before you can be challenged and it's unlikely to happen for five or six. Much can happen in that time and much can be learnt. As for any other dangers, why, if you left with me now we might be set upon by bandits in a few days and perish in the wilderness. You came out into the world to find adventure and what else have you found? If it's not as pleasant as you'd like, why, you've only discovered the reason some of us don't go out of our way to look for it. Adventures are rarely clean, neither is life. But your life has only just truly begun, don't lose heart now and wish you'd stayed at home. All this may not be as you expected, but where would the point of life be if it only turned out just as you expected? If it's the king's death that troubles you so, don't torment yourself over it. Any guilt there is rests with those who tricked you into the contest. You can learn from his death and be sorry it happened at your hands, but don't let it overwhelm you. You set out to find life and your path led you here, so accept it. Though it may seem that your load is too heavy, don't do as I did and try to escape from it, face your fate now while you're young and strong enough to cope with it. Don't think of running away because, take my word, you'll always regret it. Why look on me as your last hope Rufus? You're your own best hope. Your life is a virgin book and you're young and strong enough to fill its pages to the full. Accept all this that's fallen on you and make what you can of it. Keep your heart pure and your mind open and what great harm can come to you?'

'There,' said Lazarus lowering his voice. 'That's the advice of an old man and an onlooker. We old men are forever remembering our mistakes and because it's too late for us to do anything about them ourselves, we can only try to keep others from going the same way. Usually we give our advice in vain though, it's rarely we have the chance to open our mouths where our words will be heeded.'

Rufus burst out laughing.

'Oh, Lazarus,' he said at last when he controlled himself, 'you truly were my last hope. You've given me all the help I could ask for. But come, you're not as old as all that. I think I shall insist anyway that you visit me from time to time to make sure I'm keeping on the right track.'

'Well, perhaps I'm not too old yet to put myself to that much of a test,' said Lazarus, delighted at the effect of his words.

—X—
Aznavor's True Colours

When Lazarus left the Citadel, he kept a careful watch over his shoulder to see if he was followed. His private judgement of Aznavor was not quite as reserved as he had made out to Rufus but, having no proof and seeing no good that it would do, he had kept the depths of his suspicion to himself. This was probably just as well since Aznavor had overheard every word of their conversation.

He was no more than a hundred yards from the gate when one of the sentries left his post and quietly set out after him. Lazarus increased his pace and turned left into a crowded bazaar. For a while he threaded a devious path through the maze of the city, seeking always the places of greatest din and confusion, trying to lose himself in the multitude of faces, noises and smells. He thought he'd succeeded and stopped to survey the crowd behind him. There was no sign of a uniform. Then with a start Lazarus realised that the man was no more than a couple of paces away, his armour concealed beneath a long, striped, brown robe which he must have commandeered from one of the stalls they had passed. Lazarus resigned himself and went on more slowly, heading directly for the inn. The soldier trailed after him doggedly, changing his cloak from time to time.

There was a caravan due to leave the following day and, with no attempt at secrecy, Lazarus prepared his goods and animals and made arrangements to join it. Perhaps those who watched him would have been interested to hear some of his conversations that night after the evening meal, but whatever private words Lazarus had to say were spoken well out of earshot and only to the most trustworthy of his acquaintances.

With the first light of dawn the caravan left the stirring city, filing out through the three city gates and down the mountainside, following the road through clefts of inky shadow and ledges of brilliant morning sunshine. At the foot of the mountain they took the road that led to the distant mountains in the north-east and the lands that lay beyond.

Shortly afterwards, a well-armed squadron of soldiers set out after them.

The caravan travelled at a leisurely pace that day since they had far to go before reaching shelter again. Their escort held back out of sight, sending forward only a few scouts to shadow the travellers more closely. And thus they made their way through the shimmering, humming, dusty yellow heat of the day. If any of the travellers noticed their escort, none mentioned it and no more men than usual were posted to watch that night.

The night lay dark and moonless above the camp, the only sounds were the moaning of the wind, the rustle of dry grass and stunted bushes, and occasional snorts from the animals. The soldiers had settled themselves silently just beyond the crest of a rocky knoll and within a couple of hundred yards of the merchants.

The night passed and with the dawn, as usual, the travellers rose and prepared themselves for the day's journey. The hidden eyes in the nearby rocks silently took note of the fact that Lazarus was no longer with them. His three donkeys were now in the care of another trader and two horses were missing. The caravan filed away into the distance. The soldiers, after a fruitless search for Lazarus' trail, marched unhappily back to the city.

A week or two after Lazarus' departure, something happened which did much to clear up Rufus' opinion of Aznavor though unfortunately it did not completely put his mind at rest, for reasons which will become clear later. What took place was this:

Rufus woke in the middle of the night. His mind was instantly clear and alert as if he had caught some hint of approaching danger. He lay still, listening intently. In a few moments he heard the sound again, but it was no stealthy sound of an intruder which had woken him. The noise was deep and low, a muted rumble which seemed to travel more through the fabric of the building than the air. Rufus raised his head and looked around. His apartment was empty. The moon slanted its clear rays at a shallow angle through the western windows, their white curtains billowed in a gentle breeze. He rose cautiously and pulled on some clothes before setting off with his sword to see what was going on.

The noise continued intermittently. Though it was difficult to gauge the direction from which it came, it led Rufus to the little door he never used, the one leading to the top gallery in the great arch, housing the giant statue of the Smiling One, the door by which Aznavor sometimes visited him. All the entrances to the king's apartments were constantly guarded save this one, which was simply locked from within at night. The reflected light of the moon shone full upon its sturdy cedar panels, so before proceeding further Rufus had to return to his room to draw the curtains across the western window.

The moon hung just above the horizon. Caught full in its magical, silvery light, Rufus almost forgot what he was doing. With a drape in each hand he stood as if in a trance, gazing straight at the moon's face with its mouth open in a wordless cry. It crossed his mind that perhaps he was in a dream. Then a rumble from behind drew him back to the present. He pulled himself together and closed out the light, returned to the little door and unlocked it as silently as possible, then slid like a shadow out onto the gallery where he was met with an astonishing sight.

Below him, the giant statue's head was twisted on its shoulders so that it was looking up and slightly behind it to a spot on the seventh gallery almost directly opposite Rufus. What was more astonishing was that this twisting was achieved as naturally as if the statue was made of flesh and blood, not solid stone. Standing at the spot on the seventh gallery, opposite and slightly to the left of Rufus, stood Aznavor.

The only illumination of this bizarre scene came from the yellow light spilling out of Aznavor's open door on the left, since the courtyard on the right was almost completely in shadow.

Aznavor and the giant statue were having a conversation, it was the statue's voice which had woken Rufus.

'You're not very grateful for this opportunity I've kindly given you to talk,' Aznavor was saying. 'Nor for the news I've brought. You're lucky that it pleases me to hear what remarks you may have to make about it.'

'What cause have I to be grateful?' asked the statue. 'You've only come to gloat and air your pride at having imprisoned me here in this stone. It's not my need you're satisfying but your own. Your deeds are so treacherous that I'm the only one you can boast to about them. Besides, I don't need you to tell me what's going on in the world. I may be helpless but I'm not yet blind.'

'You'll have seen then,' sneered Aznavor, 'that the brown gods are on the move again, and what's more, that they're under my power?'

'You flatter yourself Aznavor. It's not your power they're under but mine, my power which you have merely perverted to your own evil ends. Do you really believe they would do your bidding for a moment if they were not still restrained by my influence?'

'You're playing with words, my friend, what does it matter if they do my bidding because of my control over you or for any other reason, what difference does it make as long as they do what I want? I'll tell you something else though, they're going to enjoy themselves more under me than they ever did under you. Wait till they realise that and then we'll see who's their true master.'

'You'll strangle yourself in the webs of your own cunning, Aznavor. You think you know so much, but you're like a child playing with fire when you meddle in these matters. Your cunning may have caught me off guard because I least suspected it in you, but even the least of the brown gods is infinitely more learned in cunning than you. If ever you should lead them back to the old ways and break the hold I had on them, they'll tear you to pieces in an instant like hawks with a swallow.'

'Don't try to scare me, O Great Compassionate One, it doesn't suit you, also I think perhaps that more than one of us suffers from pride. I'm not such a babe as you imagine and what do your excuses matter when it's deeds that count in this world? However you put it, I have you trapped and with a click of my fingers I can freeze you as before or have you march around the city like an elephant, trumpeting me as your new god. What is that but power? As the proverb says: "He who rules the master rules also the slaves." If I control you, what have I to fear from your brown gods? But come, Smiling One, enough of this fruitless banter, what do you think of our new king?'

'I pity him for falling into your hands, but who knows, he may yet prove to be your stumbling-block. For that matter any of your schemes may, for half the time you don't know what you're doing. Have you forgotten that you do not rule me? You only have me imprisoned. You can use some of my powers for your own ends perhaps, you can make my prison pronounce your thoughts and do your bidding, but you don't rule me just as you can never be master of the brown gods.'

'You pedantic old fossil!' shouted Aznavor. 'If I hear much more of this I'll silence you for another year, if not for good. What does it matter if it's only your form that does what I say? To the people you and your statue are the same, what the statue says, so says the Smiling One. If I use your powers then I'm your ruler, what are you but your powers? If the brown gods obey my commands then I'm their ruler, not you. I conquered you because I'm stronger than you just as you were stronger than them!'

There followed a pause during which the two stared at each other, Aznavor livid and breathing heavily, the enormous face below him sad.

'Come, Aznavor,' said the Smiling One at last, 'it's not too late for you to undo your intrigues and hope for a little mercy. Release me and give me back my powers. You have no hope of succeeding in your ambitions. As far as I can see all your paths lead to ruin. For your own sake if for no better reason, you must abandon these schemes.'

Aznavor seemed to have recovered his temper. He sneered: 'You must think me a fool, O Wise One. You don't really think I'll give up so easily that which I've worked so hard and so long to gain? I'm not rushing into any doom, my patience is almost equal to yours, you old sluggard. Here I've had you imprisoned for years and does anyone suspect? All the people feel is that your creeping softness is taking on a new edge. They feel changes all right, they feel the brown gods growing more active, but has it occurred to anyone that it's because they have a new master? Not at all. You'll see, they'll go back to their old ways as if you'd never existed. They'll do everything I wish of them in your name and the names of our kings who from now on, you can be sure of it, will do only what I want them to do.

'But I grow weary of talking to you. You have nothing to say that interests me and for all your great age you've learned little wit. Back to sleep, you old fossil!' Aznavor clicked his fingers. The statue's head turned back to face out into the courtyard and its back straightened. The features of its face composed themselves, settled into their normal expression of smiling serenity and froze. The giant statue now looked as solid and immovable as ever.

Aznavor grinned unpleasantly then strode on his short legs back to his rooms. With the closing of his door, the great archway fell into darkness.

Rufus groped his way back through the little door and locked and bolted it behind him. He went to the western windows and drew back the drapes to find that the moon had set and the night was lit only by the thousands of stars in the cloudless sky above.

If during the night he had not been sure whether he was really awake, in the morning Rufus was even more uncertain. For this reason his view of Aznavor was not completely settled by the events he had witnessed. In the clear, solid light of day the whole incident did seem rather improbable. He went and stood on the gallery overlooking the cross-legged statue and it was as concrete as ever. It was difficult to imagine it turning and speaking like a living being.

There were, however, two points in favour of believing that it had not been a dream. The first was that in this city, where oozing liquid could form itself within minutes into a solid stone statue, a kind of reversal was not quite out of the question. The second point was that in the morning, when he went to the little door, he found it bolted as he remembered doing the night before; normally, as far as he knew, it was only locked with a key. He was not absolutely certain on this second point however, and so could not quite convince himself of the reality of that curious interview. Yet of one thing he was sure—dream or reality, it would take much to convince him of Aznavor's trustworthiness.

A few nights later Rufus woke again in the middle of the night in exactly the same way. As before, he at first lay motionless, eyes open and listening intently, his heart beating like a drum tattoo. This time there was an intruder in the room. Close at hand, out of sight behind him, someone was stealthily approaching the bed, betraying themselves only by irregular, stifled breathing. The breathing came closer and closer till it was right beside the bed. Then there came a sharp intake of breath which was held. Rufus hurled himself from the bed just as a blade slashed down and split the pillow where his head had been lying. With a shrill cry the shadowy assailant leaped across the bed after Rufus, but scooping up a small table Rufus turned and crashed it down on the hand which held the blade. The sword clattered away over the stone floor and came to rest on a carpet in a glittering pool of moonlight.

Rufus leapt onto his attacker before he recovered and after a brief struggle, subdued him. Then he dragged the person across to the balcony, picking up the sword from the floor as they went. With his foot he projected the assassin headfirst through the windows into the corner of the balcony where he lay still, face hidden in his arms. Rufus thought at first that he must be unconscious, having struck his head against the stone, but then he noticed the shoulders faintly convulsing. The intruder was crying.

Rufus relaxed against the arch of the window, though he still held the sword poised in readiness.

'Come,' he said at last, since his attacker showed no sign of moving. 'Let's see your face and hear your reasons before I call the guard.'

The huddled figure uncovered its face and raised itself on one elbow to look up at him.

The moon was full and high in the sky, the light it cast on the scene seemed almost as bright as day. For a moment Rufus thought it was a woman he had caught. The person below him wore only a simple tunic, the arms and legs were bare and hairless, the face smooth and gentle in profile, tears still glistened in the eyes. When the person spoke however, he knew it was no woman but a lad of fourteen or fifteen.

'Damn you!' cried the youth tremulously. 'I would have had you if only I hadn't hesitated!'

Rufus was lost for words. Though he had only just turned nineteen himself, the lad seemed to him little more than a boy. He couldn't bring himself to call for the guard right away, since it would almost certainly mean a speedy death for the other.

'Stand up,' he ordered. The youth did so, looking around as if for some possible avenue of escape. 'I should forget it,' Rufus told him. 'Out there it's a hundred feet to the ground and this way you'd have your own sword to contend with.' The youth looked down over the balcony edge anyway, perhaps weighing up whether the mercies he was likely to receive there were preferable to those of the palace guards.

He was four or five inches shorter than Rufus and had long, dark, hair tied back from his face with a leather thong. He was sturdily built despite his hermaphroditic air. He turned and glared resentfully at Rufus without a trace of repentance.

'What's your name?' asked Rufus.

'Why should I tell you?'

'Because if you won't talk, all I can do is hand you over to the guard right away.'

'Nalna,' said the lad, 'Nalna's my name for what it's worth.'

'Why did you try to kill me?'

'It's the least you deserve!'

'Why do you say that?'

'You killed our king! The kindest, most just king we've had. He would have been the greatest if it hadn't been for you. What more reason do you want?'

Now here was a complication. How could Rufus be angry with the boy? He moved to one side and sat on the balcony's edge, seeming to relax his guard whilst in fact remaining perfectly alert.

'Sit down, Nalna,' he said, 'and don't try anything for the moment, I think we have something to discuss before deciding what to do with you. First of all, tell me how you got in here without being stopped.'

Nalna remained standing and replied rather sullenly: 'I came down from the roof. The door was open, I guessed it would be. They say you spend much time up there, it's not as hard to get to as you might imagine. I also heard that you keep no guard within your chambers. It was the obvious way to come. I brought a rope so that if the door was locked I could climb down to one of the windows. Oh, if only I hadn't been so slow!'

'Why do you want so much to kill me?' asked Rufus again.

Nalna flashed angry, deeply hurt eyes at him, but said nothing.

'Did you know the king then?' asked Rufus.

'Know him? How could I know him, being no more than a servant in the city. I loved him, he was the greatest of our people. I used to see him sometimes when I was sent here to the Citadel by my master. He even spoke to me once, asked how old I was and then told me to come back when I was older and he'd make me a page in his service. No-one else in his place would do such a thing.'

After a pause, while he digested this, Rufus asked: 'What do you expect will happen to you now, Nalna?'

'Why, you'll have my head cut off, of course.'

'Aren't you afraid?'

'Perhaps I am, perhaps not, that's my business. I wouldn't mind if only I'd done the job. Then at least something would have been gained for the price of my head.'

'Revenge?'

'Why not?'

Now, at this point Rufus realised that here, in the form of this would-be assassin, was a potentially true and trustworthy friend. If only he could somehow convert him from this obsession with killing him, but how was he to go about it?

'Come, Nalna, let me tell you my tale and perhaps you'll be less anxious to see me dead.'

Nalna looked slightly puzzled. 'Why should you want to excuse yourself to me?' he asked. 'What does it matter to you now, you have my sword and armed men within call, your skin is whole, what more do you want? Besides, what could you say that would interest me?'

Rufus frowned. This was not going to be a simple matter. Then he had an idea.

'Come,' he said. 'We're going up to the roof. You walk in front and don't try anything, I'll be right behind you.'

Together they went up the stairs to the paved rooftop. Nalna's shoulders were drawn back slightly as if half-expecting any moment to feel the blade. This was his only sign of fear however, and he carried himself with stiff pride. They went to the pavilion where, as on the balcony, Rufus made him sit on the floor in a corner where he could not make any sudden attempt to escape.

'Well,' said Rufus when they were settled. 'Now I'm going to make a bargain with you. You promise to hear out my story without trying to escape and in return I'll give you your freedom. You can go back the way you came. Even without trusting me you can see that given only a hundred yard start you'll have a fair chance of escaping. All right? Do you agree?'

Nalna looked puzzled again but nodded readily enough. The stiffness of his posture relaxed perceptibly as hope for the future crept back into his heart. He looked around him as someone might on awaking from a stifling dream. Beyond the arches of the pagoda, beneath the moon and speckled dome of the sky, the world lay vast and still. The desert had been transformed into a sea of silver and the distant mountains into a shore of promise.

By the time Rufus came to the end of his story, the moon was almost resting on the mountains to the west. Nalna's face was in shadow.

'Well,' asked Rufus, 'is anything changed by my story?'

'If what you say is true,' replied Nalna slowly, 'then it changes everything. But how do I know I can believe you?'

Rufus wished he could see Nalna's face, because now was the moment he had to take a risk. 'If what I've said already hasn't convinced you,' said Rufus, 'then further words would be wasted. You must judge for yourself whether I speak the truth or not.' Then he reversed the sword and tossed it across the pagoda where it clattered to rest at Nalna's feet, within easy reach of his hand. Then Rufus moved away from the entrance and sat down on a ledge. The boy rose and moved to stand between Rufus and the entrance, the sword in his hand, his back to the moon.

'So I have to judge for myself, do I?' he said. His voice firm and clear. He raised the sword and came forward, stopping just out of Rufus' reach, his left hand held before him as if to ward off any possible attack and the blade poised above Rufus' shoulders.

'If I think this is some kind of trick,' said Nalna, 'my nerve won't fail me this time, you know.' Though nervous, Rufus betrayed no sign of it. He wondered for a moment what had made this seem such a good idea.

Nalna's arm moved, Rufus closed his eyes and the sword clanked to the floor for the third time that night.

'I must sit down,' said Nalna and seated himself on the ledge beside Rufus, his hand trembling. Rufus leant his head back against the stone and took a deep breath of cool night air.

'Phew!' he exclaimed. 'You had me worried for a moment.'

Nalna laughed. 'That makes two of us, but how else was I to make sure of you?'

They sat together in silence looking westward at the sinking moon. When it had quite set Nalna said: 'Well, what now? Shall I leave?'

'You can stay if you like.'

'Stay?'

'You said you were going to be the king's page, well you can still do that if you don't mind having me as your king.'

'I wouldn't be able to respect you, you know,' said Nalna, 'not in the same way I did the real king, I mean. I respect you well enough as a person for what you've just done, but not as a king. You're not different enough from me. No wait, I'm not expressing myself very well. What I mean is yes, I'd like to stay, but I can't serve you in the way I'd have served king Gamil, not now I know your story. I can't love you in the same way but I like you well enough. If I stay as your servant I'll call you lord or whatever title is needed, but remember that I'll know who you really are. If you accept me on those terms then I'll gladly stay.'

'Well,' said Rufus, holding out his hand, 'those terms seem fair enough to me, in fact I couldn't wish for any better. Shake hands on it, Master Nalna, and welcome to the Citadel.'

And so, in this way Rufus gained an invaluable friend, setting at the same time an interesting problem for Aznavor who couldn't for the life of him puzzle out where the boy had come from.

—XI—
The Golden Wheel

MEANWHILE, RUFUS had not been forgotten by his four friends in the city of the waterfall, nor by the old blind woman. Shortly after the events of the last chapter, the five of them were gathered in their kitchen for a meal, very much as we saw them before.

The evening was warm and the windows and doors were wide open to catch the slightest breeze. The fire had been allowed to die down to a pile of glowing embers which bathed the room in a pleasant, ruddy glow. The only other source of light was a single candle in one of the opposite corners of the room, whose clear yellow flame flickered and danced in the breeze. Chrysol, Emra, Nuoma and Cornelius sat along the sides of the table, dressed as usual in their characteristic colours; the old lady sat at the head, facing the fire. During and after the meal she recounted the tale of Rufus' adventures since leaving home. When she had finished they sat on for a while in silence, digesting the news and the meal together with the aid of rich red wine from an earthenware flagon.

Emra broke the silence at last:

'Tell us mother, what has become of Rufus' father?'

'Ah,' replied the old lady, 'now there's another curious tale. Shortly after Rufus left, his father suddenly sold up his house and business and went off into the world himself to look for his son. I met him with his donkey just before they left the city.'

'And did you tell him in which direction to go?'

'I did. I told him that by a strange fortune I had recently met a young man who sounded just like his son and who had left with a trader's caravan bound for the north not a week previously.'

'You didn't!' cried Emra, rather shocked.

'I did,' affirmed the old lady with an almost roguish grin. 'What use would it have been to put him on the right trail? Rufus as yet thinks nothing of his father, nor even considers the chance that there was anything wrong in the way he left home. In time perhaps his thoughts will turn back and he'll wish to see him again, but that's unlikely to happen for some time yet. What would he have to say to his father if they did meet now, and what's more important, what would his father have to say to him? Besides, though I doubt if he'd agree if he heard me say it, the travelling and the search will do him no harm. Quite the reverse in fact, it will do him a great deal of good, it will bring him fully to life again, which he has not been since the death of his wife. Put your heart at rest, Emra dear, when the time is ripe he'll find Rufus again. In fact I have a bit of a plan to help it come about.

'You recall Rufus' companion on his journey, the travelling merchant named Lazarus? Well, when he slipped away from the city of brown gods he had it in mind to come here. For the best of reasons he's been following a rather roundabout route, but he'll soon be arriving. Though he said nothing to Rufus himself, he has it in mind to visit his father and, without revealing too much, to reassure him of Rufus' safety such as it is. He, too, felt sympathy for a father who loses his son. Well, this is where you four can help. When Lazarus arrives and finds the father gone, I want you to engage him on business which will take him to the north. If we arrange for him to follow the same route as Rufus' father, they're sure to meet up sooner or later and then we can leave them to their own devices. It will be a while before Lazarus feels safe in returning to his home town, but I've little doubt that when he does so he'll take the father with him and that Rufus will then be equally glad to see them both.'

There followed another meditative silence, broken this time by Cornelius who said with a slight frown: 'I feel uneasy, mother. It makes me restless to think of young Rufus in the hands of this jackal, Aznavor. Is his life not in constant danger as long as this remains so, and could we not perhaps do something about it? We've lived here in peace and quiet long enough, I feel the need for action. Young Rufus alone is no match for this man and what makes it worse is that even if he were, he would not know how to manage without him. Do you not think, mother, that we should visit our young friend and help him settle his affairs?'

'Ah, Cornelius,' smiled the old lady, 'I was wondering how this peaceful life was affecting you. So you're restless are you? Well, perhaps we can do something about that, for it's not only to talk of Rufus that I've come here tonight. But first of all my answer is no, it would not be a good idea for you to visit Rufus. You'll have your chance to help him in time, though probably not in the way you imagine and certainly not yet. You may be right in supposing yourselves to be a fair match for our friend Aznavor, and if the worst comes to the worst you may yet have your chance with him, but for the moment we must let things be. Let Rufus find and test his own strength, it would be better for him to match Aznavor with his own wits than with yours. Besides, I've had my reasons for persuading you to rest here these last months. I think the time is ripe for you to learn something more about yourselves and that, in the long run, will be worth more to you, and to Rufus if he should need your help, than any rash adventures at the moment. Be patient, Cornelius, now is the time for learning, not doing.

'Now, where shall I begin?' the old blind lady paused thoughtfully and took a sip of her wine before continuing. 'Well, you know of course that I've always followed your lives with great attention, since long before you met me and in fact since the time you were all in your cradles. I watched you and followed your growth as I have done with Rufus these last months. I watched you come together as children and grow up together, saw you win and give away fortunes which others would have risked their lives for, followed you in thought during your adventures among strange peoples and in unknown places. All this time I've watched and hardly interfered. All this time I've been waiting for the day you'll have grown wise and experienced enough to learn something I've known from the beginning, something concerning your own true natures which you need to know if you're to fulfil your lives properly. Now I think the day has come. But I'll say no more, words at this point would be idleness, it's time for seeing and learning. Let's go upstairs.'

The old lady took her knobbed walking stick in hand and made to rise from the table. Chrysol quickly pushed back his chair and came to offer her his arm. The other three rose also with slightly puzzled expressions, and together they mounted the stairs to the topmost room of the house.

From the outside of that pleasant house it could be seen that one part of it rose a storey above the rest of the building like a square tower. Each face of this top storey was a gable-end containing two tall narrow windows side by side which rose and ended in graceful pointed arches. The ridges of the roof thus made by the gables were in the form of a cross which reflected itself in the shape of the room below.

The room thus had four alcoves, the walls of which rose straight from the floor and then curved to match the slope of the tiles, giving an effect rather like the vaulting of a chapel. Each alcove with its pair of pointed windows was decorated principally in one of the colours favoured by the four who lived in the house; the one facing north being blue, the one south green, east red and west yellow. From the central point in the ceiling where all the curved walls met, hung a lamp. Four more lamps were suspended by each pair of windows. Beneath the central lamp, in the very centre of the carpeted floor, stood the table Rufus had found and bought from the robbers by the river. It glistened in the lamplight like rich and aged gold.

In one of the angles of this cross-shaped room arose a spiral stair from the floor below. In the opposite angle stood a tall, dark and intricately carved chair. A small brazier filled the air with the sweet smell of incense and the rich curtains were drawn against the night.

This then, was the room to which the five repaired. The old lady sat in the chair while the four stood, one on each side of the table with their backs to the alcoves, each one framed by their own characteristic colour. As on many previous occasions, they rested their hands gently on the surface of the table, fingers splayed and lightly touching those of both of their neighbours. The room was filled with silence. They looked down at the centre of the table and after a while, in a soft, murmuring voice, Nuoma started reciting the first verse of the rhyme inscribed on the table and in turn the others followed suit. The gentle rhythm of the words flowed round and round the room hypnotically and as it did so, very gradually, the room seemed to melt away into darkness, leaving the five of them and the table alone in a vague undefined gloom, lit only by the five lamps shining like planets.

Then the darkness seemed to move and swirl like fog in an eddy of fresh wind. Misty, vague, disquieting shapes formed and clustered around them like faint dancing ghosts, but the five took no notice and continued with their low chant. Then the shapes disappeared and all was again dark, still and empty. Then a dim, deep blue glow penetrated the darkness and surrounded them, blue like a clear summer night seen through the window of a pitch dark room. This blue light grew stronger and stronger while the five twinkling lights grew dim and faded from sight, leaving the five of them alone with their table and chair, suspended in the blue glow as in the midst of an ocean. Each was perfectly aware of the others and of everything around them although they did not lift their eyes from the centre of the table. All this so far was as they had experienced it many times before, but from this point onwards everything was new.

First, there streamed outwards from a point above their heads, a million speckles of pale blue, spreading outwards to surround them in a swirling, sweeping pattern like the bubbles of a splashing river seen through a kaleidoscope, ever changing and rushing but moving also in graceful symmetry. The speckles gradually merged into threads which turned and twisted and curled in ever-changing and ever more complex patterns. Then, from that point above their heads, something else appeared against the swirling blue, something small and distant and golden. Without raising their eyes they were as aware of this as if, like insects, they had eyes pointing in every direction. The golden object drew closer and soon they could see that it was a golden wheel revolving in the air. But this was not all, for standing against the wheel, radiating from its centre and with their legs intertwined in a curious and somehow meaningful fashion, were four people. I say people for want of a better word, for their form may have been human, but there was something strange, unearthly and glowing about them, as if they were not lit by any external sun or moon but by a light radiating from themselves. These four were clothed, like those below, each in a particular colour.

With gasps of astonishment, the four at the table raised their heads and looked directly at the Golden Wheel. The four radiant beings smiled down enigmatically at them from faces as much like those of Chrysol, Emra, Nuoma and Cornelius as if they were looking out of a mirror.

Then, as the Wheel revolved, so the ever-changing pattern in the background changed colour from blue to red to green to yellow and back again to blue, and so on in succession in a symphony of light and colour and form.

The hearts of the four were hammering furiously, though whether in wonder or fear or some kind of combination of the two, I doubt if they themselves could have told. Then a further change came for, appearing out of the distance in the same way as the Wheel itself, came four more, smaller discs which grew and stationed themselves above the heads of each of the four on the Wheel. There they revolved, keeping their places like moons around a planet, each a different colour.

How long this vision lasted I cannot say. To the four it seemed an infinitely long time, yet when it faded they felt that the end had come too soon. The swirls and revolving wheels above them melted into a still, dark blue glow which itself faded into vague darkness from which emerged five star-like lamps and the outlines of the room itself, as though from a mist. And then, everything was as it had been in the beginning.

The four blinked at each other and then looked at the old woman in mute astonishment; and again, how long this state lasted they could not tell.

At last the blind lady rose from her chair, smiling gently. She kissed each of them on the cheek and led them downstairs again to the kitchen. There she sat them down and filled their cups with red wine, and thus they sat far into the night without a word being spoken. If ever one of them seemed about to speak, the old lady silently reprimanded them with a finger on her smiling lips. Not until the following day did she give them any kind of explanation.

This is perhaps a suitable point for me to try and sketch a little more of the history of the previous involvement of the four with the table, as it may shed a little more light on what the old lady had to say to them the following day. I fear it may be a rather rough and incomplete sketch but I hope you will bear with me.

Well, as we have seen earlier, it was Nuoma who first led the four to the table in the city's underground passages. It was she also who led them to put it in a disused room of her home and later showed them how to make use of it.

When they first stood around it in the manner we have just seen, staring at its centre point and murmuring the inscribed verses, nothing much happened at first. Then the room grew dark, and faint, wraith-like shapes gathered around them. These shapes were too faint to be seen when looked at directly but, when they discovered that it was not necessary to raise their eyes from the table to be aware of what was around them, the wraiths grew clearer and took on a more solid outline. This was as much as they saw the first time and it did not last long, but it was enough to excite their further curiosity.

Over the years following, they continued their investigations from time to time, and as they did so their experiences gradually changed. At first they took the apparitions to be ghosts or something similar, but as they grew to see them more clearly, they found that this was not the case. I'm not quite sure how to describe them, the creatures were fantastic, often monstrous, half-formed abortions of creation, things which haunt madmen's visions, glimpses of Chaos, the sphere of shards on the edge of the outer darkness.

It would be reasonable to expect that sights which torment madmen would strike at least a certain amount of terror into their hearts, yet this was not so. They felt as if they stood in a magic circle which the creatures were powerless to cross. It was as if the table and the ritual which enabled them to see these things, at the same time protected them from any harm that might come of it. All they felt was a fascination with the endless profusion, even though much of what they saw was rather grotesque. This at least was more or less the case with all of them except Emra who found the sights repellent. Still, she too persisted, partly for the sake of the others and partly because Nuoma assured her that this was not the end of the exercise, that these experiences were leading to something of real value to all of them, that there was no other way to reach that end. What exactly the end was she could not say, but they were all used to trusting her convictions.

One of the peculiarities of these experiences was that, although at the time they saw these things as concretely as the normal everyday world, afterwards they quickly slipped the memory unless they were sketched or written down. Another peculiarity was that, when they did sketch or record what they had seen, they were struck by the complete disconnectedness and lack of any kind of sense in the visions. Grotesque, phantasmagoric, comic or even beautiful in a strange way, they could see all these things here and there, but the whole was completely jumbled and random. Nothing remained still or the same for longer than a few moments but these changes, far from revealing any kind of pattern, only compounded the confusion. Perhaps this partly accounts for the difficulty they had in remembering afterwards.

In time these glimpses of Chaos would be followed by the clear blue light we have seen, and later still by the other three colours. But to describe them as being bathed in light does not quite do justice to their experiences, because together with the light they were washed in sensations and feelings, a subtle ambiance which depended on the colour and also a powerful sense of buoyancy and freedom of mind.

Each of the colours had a distinctive ambiance, and this in fact is how the four came to choose their own colours, the colours whose mood most matched their own general approach to life. It's not surprising therefore, since she always led them in these experiences, that Nuoma chose blue for her own colour and that this was always the colour they most frequently saw.

It must be admitted that, since they had a certain amount of control in the matter, at first they often chose not to move into the sphere of these colours but to remain in the level of grotesque fantasy. They often did this despite feeling that it was a rather backward step. I suppose it was the emptiness of the colours as compared to the rich profusion of the creatures, the strangeness which excited the curiosity and inflamed the imagination. In time though, they did move on and learnt to value the stillness of the colours more highly. They noticed the curiously refreshing effect they had, a soothing, healing effect. Also they noticed that, although they were unaware of any thoughts or decisions at the time, when the colours faded they found that the solutions to many problems which had unsettled their minds before, now seemed perfectly obvious. I believe this is similar to the effects of some kinds of meditation, but with one important difference; during these experiences they were perfectly aware of each other at the same time as whatever was happening around them. At times it was as if the four of them became one person. So, after a while, they tended to ignore the fantastic creatures beyond the extent to which they intruded themselves.

This was how matters stood when the table was stolen from them during their absence from the city on some expedition.

After the loss of the table they continued these meditations as best they could, but although they often reached the point of being bathed in light, the experience was harder to gain and less frequently successful. When they had their table returned to them by Rufus, their delight was well justified for they rediscovered the joy and ease of those early experiences.

The morning following the strange events, just described, saw the old blind lady and the four friends gathered in the room above the kitchen. This room was spacious, cool and airy. The tall windows faced northwards, overlooking the garden, and through them flowed a warm, scent-laden breeze. The walls and ceiling were completely whitewashed and against them hung a few European tapestries and Chinese ink paintings. The room was sparingly furnished with light furniture, mats and cushions.

Around a low table by the windows were four large cushions and a wickerwork chair. On the table itself stood a large pot of scented tea and several small, handle-less cups. Here the five sat sipping the clear, golden, unsweetened tea, replenishing the cups frequently from the large pot, a habit they had picked up during their travels in the Far East. Not a word had yet been spoken about the events of the evening before. It was Chrysol who first broached the subject:

'Well, mother,' he said. 'Perhaps now you can tell us what and who it was we saw last night.'

The old lady smiled. 'Yes, perhaps it is time dear, but don't expect me to explain everything. I'll tell you no more than you need to be going on with. The Golden Wheel is what you saw, but I expect that what you most want to know is who the four beings were and why they looked exactly like you? Yes? Well, I'll begin there.

'Have I not always told you that when we're born we forget our true natures, that the main purpose of our lives is to rediscover and realise them? Surely you did not think I was merely using figures of speech? What you saw last night was precisely that, your own true natures as they exist in the timeless sphere. Perhaps you thought that what you saw was some kind of reflection of yourselves, well the exact opposite is the case. You four are a reflection of them. In each of you was the essence of one of them planted when you were conceived, the essence but not the memory or knowledge they have, you'll only receive that completely when you merge again with them. This is what I mean when I say we have to rediscover ourselves. It is true for everyone, but most particularly for you four, because you were so much closer to your true natures to begin with than most people.

'If this is so, you may be wondering why you never knew it before, or at least why you didn't recognise it when you met as children, why it should have often seemed to you that you were the most unsuited of all your companions. Well, my answer is that that was the whole point, that is why you were kept in ignorance from the beginning. The harmony of the Golden Wheel is not that of like with like, which is at best a tepid harmony, but that of the equal balancing of opposites which is true harmony. Because it is a balance of opposites which is the most difficult to gain. Human nature does not like to face this, it prefers to believe that like goes best with like because life seems so much simpler that way, even though it doesn't work. People prefer not to face the difficulty of judging the difference between things that are different and hostile to each other, and things that are different but which could be brought into harmony, because they look much the same at first sight. This is why, in your early days, you were so often in conflict and why it seemed to you that you were the most ill-matched of friends. It took friction and conflict to balance your opposite natures, not until that was done did you achieve something like a reflection of the Golden Wheel in this world. When opposites are joined in harmony they produce something much stronger than the opposites in themselves; so it was with you in a purely human way when you came together, and so it was with the Golden Wheel.'

There followed a meditative pause broken by Emra who voiced the feelings of all the four: 'What you say mother makes me feel suddenly very small, like a child again. It's as if,' she broke off and hunted for a phrase. 'It's as if I were a small branch on a tree. The tree grows by a wall which has a small hole and the branch grows through the hole, knowing nothing of the tree on the other side of the wall and thinking itself to be a whole tree, bathing in the sun and wind and looking down on the world very pleased and self-contented. Then one day the wall tumbles down and the branch realises it's no more than the smallest of hundreds growing from a great tree-trunk the size of which it had never even thought possible.'

The old lady laughed pleasantly. 'Well spoken, Emra, and I'm happy that it's small you feel and not suddenly very large. It can surely do you no harm to feel small, not you four before whom the obstacles of this world melt like sand in a thunderstorm.'

'Perhaps,' she continued, 'you also see why I told Cornelius that this was not the time to go to Rufus' aid. It was both for your own sakes and his. For your own because you need time free from action to learn more about your own natures and that of the Golden Wheel. For Rufus' sake because, like you, he has his own destiny to work out and it would not necessarily help to remove all dangers and difficulties from his path. He's in a dangerous enough position all right and there's no doubt of Aznavor's evil, yet it would still be best to leave him to discover his own strength to defeat Aznavor, even though he runs the risk of failing and perishing in doing so.'

She paused and Chrysol interposed: 'But about the Golden Wheel, if they, or we, already existed in a state of perfect harmony, where was the need for us to recreate it, to recreate a shadow of it in ignorance of what we were doing? Also you seem to suggest that we might have failed. Well, before all this we would have agreed readily enough that it was the greatest good fortune that brought and kept us together, but how does this fit with what you've now told us?'

'Hm,' said the old lady. 'I can see that our discussion is going to get a deal more difficult before it gets easier. It's a matter of time. In this world time flows in sequence, in a spiral sequence, but there it is rather different. There the Golden Wheel can exist at the same time as its complete opposite, at the same time as complete conflict between the Four. So the causes of conflict and the development of harmony are not so clear. Here in this world you can only be in either one state or the other. When in one state, the other exists only as a possibility and as you move backwards and forwards between one and the other, so the causes of harmony and discord become clear. When your time here is over and you return to them, like rivers to the sea, so you'll carry back all you'll have learned.'

As their discussion did indeed grow more difficult, before it grew easier, as it became highly metaphysical and not quite relevant to our story, not yet anyway, it is perhaps best to pass over the next couple of hours with a nimble leap to Chrysol's final question of the day. He had been observing the old lady for a while with a concentrated gaze and a puzzled frown. At last he brought himself to voice his doubt:

'Tell us mother,' he asked, 'in all this talk you have, as ever, said nothing about yourself. Where exactly do you fit into the picture?'

'Ah,' she replied, smiling mysteriously. 'It will be an interesting day when you find the answer to that question.'

—XII—
The Haunted Hills

AFTER MAKING friends with Nalna, Rufus set his mind to work on the problem of what exactly to do with himself. Any prospect of actually having a hand in ruling the country remained as distant as ever, but he felt a need for action, to justify his life in some way and to prepare himself for any possible treachery by Aznavor.

Aznavor, meanwhile, was furthering his own plans with great speed and energy. By a process of bribery, intimidation, subtle poisoning and his favourite method of bringing about the disgrace of his enemies, he was gradually eliminating all opposition to himself within the Citadel. Many of the lords were unaware of or indifferent about his ambitions and of the others, most did not dare openly oppose him and the rest were either making secret plans to go into exile or hoping against hope that their opposition had escaped Aznavor's notice.

Rufus' first move was to resume his weapon training. Part of his motives for doing so may have been a slight uneasiness that he had not won the contest with the previous king entirely on his own merits, but besides this it was the one avenue of progress that seemed open to him. So, after assuring himself that he was trustworthy, he enlisted the aid of his former mentor Shasta, the gruff old sergeant who had trained him for the contest. Under careful questioning it seemed almost certain that, like Lazarus, Shasta had played an unwitting part in Aznavor's plot. The old soldier cared nothing for politics or intrigues, nor even very much for kings. His loyalties were placed with his city and his people, his interests were solely the arts of battle and the company of his friends in the taverns at night.

This casual attitude towards the king was not uncommon among soldiers in the Citadel. Originally, of course, the kings had all been great warriors and charismatic leaders and so could automatically command great loyalty from their troops. The fortunes of the country had depended very much on each one's particular personality. Of late though, the kings had risen obscurely and not usually lasted very long, also the affairs of the country seemed little affected by them. To this extent I suppose it could be said that Aznavor's doings had been noticed by those in the Citadel below the level of the lords, but none of them were fully conscious of the changes nor did they reflect on possible causes of them. They went through the forms and motions of complete loyalty, but in fact the Citadel soldiers were waiting for something by which to judge Rufus, some sign of character to make their loyalty either more or less than pure duty.

So in fact, in his opposition to Aznavor, Rufus began in exactly the right way. He and Nalna trained daily in the same yard where his training had first begun or else on the paved roof above the king's apartments. They were both apt pupils and gained rapidly in sturdiness, strength and proficiency.

'All you need now, my lord,' said Shasta one day after this had been going on for about a month, 'is a battle in which to test your skill. More training now can do nothing to improve you, for there are some things which only experience can teach.'

Now, the city was not at that time involved in any wars but there was still fighting work for its soldiers to do. The wilds were full of bandits in those days who liked nothing better than to find a rich, juicy caravan on the roads far from home. The duty of a city then was to keep its links with the wide world as open as was possible.

There were principally two kinds of bandit. The first were those bands of outlaws and outcasts, cut-throats and the dregs of humanity who collected in the hills by the main routes. The second were roving bands of fierce nomads on horseback who roamed from country to country with their families, sacking and plundering where they could. The first kind were the chief targets of the army's expeditions as, given the chance, they would stay in one area sacking every caravan that came their way. They were completely ruthless, sparing only those women and youths who took their fancy in order that no word of their presence should leak out and spread the alarm. The second kind, who were often remnants of the marauding hordes of the Mongol khans, were not quite as bad, as they were always on the move and were often content merely to plunder and not massacre the caravans. One of the purposes of the army expeditions though, was to keep an eye open for any band of these nomads large enough to be tempted to try their hand at sacking a prosperous city.

It was arranged therefore that Rufus and Nalna would accompany one of these expeditions and that the faithful Shasta would go with them. Old though he was growing for active soldiering, Shasta was not yet ready for a quiet retirement. He said that as a young man he had always expected to die on the battlefield and sounded almost disappointed that this had not yet happened to him.

A week or two later found the three of them sitting at night around a small, crackling camp-fire in the mountains far to the north and slightly to the east of their city. They had in fact followed the same road as Lazarus' caravan when he had made his stealthy exit from the country.

The expedition consisted basically of three units. One was a troop of soldiers disguised as rich, almost defenceless travelling merchants who acted as bait for the trap; not a very enviable duty, but in fact there were always more than enough promotion-hungry young volunteers for the job. The second was a troop of horse and camel-mounted fighters to counter any mounted attack. The third, the group which Rufus and his friends had joined, was a squad of foot-soldiers.

The mission so far had been quite successful as this road had not been patrolled for some time. Only four days out from the city they had wiped out a small and miserable band of cut-throats who had crept up on the caravan at night.

Incidentally, when, as we saw earlier, a squad of soldiers followed Lazarus out of the city after Rufus' crowning, their orders had naturally come from Aznavor. They had been carefully picked as men who would not question what they were to do. Their mission was to dispose of Lazarus some days' journey from the city and to make it look as if it was the work of just such a band as this first one the patrol had disposed of. If they had succeeded, Rufus' expedition would have provided a perfect cover for their deception.

In the foothills of the mountain range the expedition had come across stronger opposition, the decoy caravan had been attacked in broad daylight. After a fierce battle the brigands had been routed and it was the pursuit of the last remnants of their band which had led Rufus and his foot-soldiers deep into the jagged mountains to the west of the road. When night fell they had gone too far to return to their fellows and so had made camp as best they could where they found themselves.

Rufus sat a little apart from the rest of the troop in the company of Nalna and Shasta. Their small camp-fire flickered bravely in the gusts of wind. The moon was a little before the full and rode about a quarter of the way above the eastern horizon, behind a ragged veil of clouds which hung above the mountains. The clouds were massing as if for a storm though there was no smell of rain in the air. Over the plain to the south, however, where the city stood, the sky was clear and star-strewn.

'Well Shasta,' said Rufus, 'what do you think of this day's work?'

The old warrior was lightly whetting the edge of his blade on a pocket-stone. His bristled face was grim and hard like rock, deeply lined and scarred. His hair and whiskers were iron grey and streaked with white, they resisted the gusts of wind like wire wool. As somehow fitted his person, his sword was shorter, straighter and broader than was usual. His eyes smouldered in the light of the flames as if with their own inner light, the last trace of the deadly, tightly controlled passion he had shown in battle. Without pausing in his work he replied:

'I could have wished for stouter foes than these carrion to take the ache and stiffness out of my old joints, but I'll not be complaining too loud. It was the next best thing to a real battle and a fair sport for newcomers to the game like yourself, my lord. You handled yourself well, it'll not take much to make a real soldier of you. Soon you'll have to learn to command and I'm thinking you'll not do better than to take young Dornil as your teacher then.' 'Young' Dornil was the one who was directing the operation although Rufus was the leader in name. He was in fact little younger than Shasta himself but it seemed that some long-standing, friendly running argument stood between them.

'And you, young sir,' continued Shasta turning to Nalna, 'given a few years to flesh out your frame you could be a fair match for your master here. I'm thinking though that you might be cursed with a soft heart, I'm thinking it might be best for you to find another trade by which to earn your bread and to save your sword for war time.'

Rufus and Nalna shared the same rather mixed feelings for the old soldier. His bloodthirstiness in battle and casual lack of sympathy for the foe made him quite fearsome to watch at work, yet they could feel nothing intrinsically evil or even violent about him. To be fair, Shasta expected no more from his enemies than he offered them, also his battle-passion was in a curious way impersonal. He fought for his country and people, and his passion was on their behalf. Little seemed able to rouse him to anger for his own sake.

Beneath his grim and gruff exterior he seemed to have taken quite a liking to the two young men in his charge. In the heat of the battle earlier that day, when they had cornered the bandits, he had several times helped them out of tricky situations rather with the air of a blacksmith with his apprentices; stepping into the fray when they were hard-pressed, and demonstrating various techniques, then stepping aside again for them to try their own hands. Then, if he thought they were taking too long, he would shoulder them to one side and, with a barrage of precise hammer-strokes, despatch the bandits. His battle-passion was like a fiery stallion over which he held a tight rein, but from time to time he would give the fury its head.

No doubt Shasta was quite justified in his attitudes and no doubt they were quite apt for his time and situation, but neither Rufus nor Nalna thought they would ever quite acquire his professional attitude and rather ghoulish satisfaction with his trade. His praise, however, felt worth earning.

'It's a pity though,' continued Shasta after one of the long pauses which usually punctuated his conversation, 'it's a pity we let this handful slip through our fingers. They're probably no more friendly than us with any other bandits round here, but you never know.' He lapsed again into silence and worked away on his blade. He was stropping it very finely now, taking care that in renewing the edge he did not distort the shape of the blade.

Rufus looked around him at the shadowy mountainside. They were camped in a hollow scooped from the lower slopes of the mountain which raised its bare, jagged claw abruptly above them to the north-west. The upper end of the hollow cut steeply into the slope. The other sides were protected by a natural wall of boulders which had been improved by the men against any possible attack before settling for the night.

Although only on the lower slopes of this mountain, they were already high above the plain to the south, of which glimpses could be caught through the peaks of the foothills. Much of the view that way, however, was obscured by the shoulders of their own mountain.

Then Rufus noticed that the soldiers seemed restless. The place did not require much of a guard, yet most of them were at the edge of the hollow, and looking out into the night in whispering groups. Those who stayed by the fires kept their eyes averted from the flames to avoid their sight being dimmed. Rufus asked Shasta the reason for this strange behaviour.

'They think these hills are haunted,' returned Shasta looking around at them rather contemptuously. 'You'd think soldiers would know better than to waste their energy on fears of the mind when there's enough real dangers in the world.'

Shortly afterwards Rufus curled up in his blanket and went to sleep.

In the middle of the night he awoke to the muted sound of alarm all around him. Swiftly getting to his feet and unsheathing his sword, he found the camp in a flurry of confusion. The ashes of fires were being scattered and stamped out and much discussion and argument was going on in urgent whispered tones. Of Shasta there was at first no sign. Then Nalna came up.

'What's going on?' asked Rufus.

'Up there on the ridge,' said Nalna pointing. 'Some say we're about to be attacked by bandits but others think we've stirred up the demons who inhabit these parts.'

The moon by now was high in the sky, but its light showed no more than as ribbons of dirty white against the black storm clouds. The wind was fiercer than before and it felt now as if the storm was about to break any minute. On the ground all was dim and shadowy, but even so movements could be seen on the crest of the ridge above them, indistinct forms moving about and flames flickering here and there.

Then Rufus saw Shasta about ten feet away and heard him growling: 'Stand firm and man your places you superstitious fools! There's something out there all right, but if it's ghosts I'll eat my armour. Man your posts and prepare yourselves or these curs will have made ghosts out of all of you before this night's out.'

But only Shasta's immediate presence affected the men, as soon as his back was turned they became as nervous and aimless as before. On the other side of the hollow, Dornil could be heard exhorting the men in a similar way, probably with as little effect although Rufus could not see.

Then, simultaneously, the wind ripped the clouds from the face of the moon and lightning burst from the top of their mountain into the sky. The scene revealed to them was like a vision from hell, for crawling down the slope from the ridge above them came a dark, boiling, fiendish army. As the moon flooded the scene with her light, the silent army sprang to their feet and sang out a blood-chilling cry. They came swarming down the slope like a hundred thousand scorpions. Inhuman shapes they were, no more than silhouettes, silhouettes of the most fantastic brood of demons. From their wailing mouths and eyes poured flames and as they streamed down the slope, a limitless multitude sprang after them over the crest of the ridge.

With one accord the soldiers threw their weapons heedlessly to the winds and fled for their lives down the mountainside, Rufus and Nalna with them. Bringing up the rear, Rufus ran with a cringing feeling of dread piercing his neck and shoulders like ice, expecting any moment to feel inhuman limbs and talons fastening into his flesh. Like the others he ran in a blind panic, but they were not attacked from behind. The column of phantoms divided and overtook them on either side, wailing chillingly and striking dread into the hearts of any bold enough to look to the side, but not touching them.

Rufus tumbled into another hollow lower down the slope. Here a few other terrified soldiers were crouched, no more than a third of their company, but they filled the narrow space with their bodies. 'It's no good going on, they're cutting us off down below,' said some. Others were simply paralysed with fear. The hollow was surrounded on all sides by boulders, Rufus turned and looked back up the slope through a gap between two of them. There seemed to be no more of their men behind them, only a sea of black fiery phantoms dividing just above their hiding place and passing on either side. It seemed indeed as if they were surrounded and trapped. Then something prompted Rufus to put his hand under his leather jerkin and clasp the amethyst cross which hung there next to his hammering heart.

The effect of this action was remarkable. As if drenched with icy water, the chaotic turmoil of his brain was instantly stilled. For a few moments he looked out through his crack with as calm a mind as if he had been Aznavor watching this scene through the crystal ball from the safety of the Citadel.

Into this stillness of mind spoke a voice, almost as clearly as if the speaker were standing beside him in a quiet room. The voice spoke in tones he recognised though he could not for the moment place them. It was a woman's voice:

'You know what you have to do, Rufus?' asked the voice. 'You have to step out into the midst of them.'

'You must be mad,' thought Rufus in reply. His legs were shaking like jelly and fear was creeping back into his veins like poison.

'Not at all,' replied the voice calmly. 'It's you and your companions who are closest to being mad. These phantoms have no power over you at all except what your own fears give them. They cannot touch you, they cannot harm you, they can only terrify you and drive you mad. You cannot escape by running away, that is only playing into their hands. You must go the other way, you must go forward into the midst of them and grasp one of them. Step out and see.'

After a tremendous battle of will, Rufus mastered his limbs and fears. With the courage of a cornered rat he selected the most monstrous of the creatures rushing down the slope, a great bulbous grinning creature, then he leapt over

the boulders, ran up the slope and flung himself upon the creature as if over a precipice.

The grinning demon hit him like a thunderclap and Rufus fell stunned to the ground. When he recovered, moments later as it seemed, he looked out on a strangely changed world. Gone were the dark broods of fiery phantoms and gone were all traces of the storm which had been gathering. There were some ghostly forms flitting around it is true, but they were pale, almost human forms with clear features. They were dispersing, disappearing behind rocks and ridges or simply melting into the ground. As they did so they looked grinningly towards Rufus, but not with the evil expressions of the former horde, their grins were mischievous, almost impish. Of the storm there was no trace at all. The sky was clear and serene and a gentle, dry breeze whispered over the slopes. The mountains, rocks and earth were crisply outlined by the radiant moon.

When the pale wraiths had all disappeared, Rufus rose painfully and looked around at the empty landscape. There was no sign of any of his fellow-soldiers. He limped over to the boulders and the little hollow which had been their refuge, but found it deserted. Puzzled, he looked around him again at the grim mountains and the glimpses of the plain rolling away south towards the horizon like a silver sea. In doing so, his gaze was caught by a most curious sight.

Some way further down the mountain's slope, on the southern flank, the ground levelled out for a space. In the centre of this area rose a small hillock and to the south of this lay a smaller pool of water in the centre of which was a tiny circular island about five feet in diameter. The pool surrounded the island with a ring of water about three feet wide and spilled down the southern slope in a little stream which soon lost itself among the rocks. The island and the ground by the pool were carpeted with lush grass.

All this, though curious enough in itself for such bare, dry terrain, was not in itself what attracted Rufus' attention; for on the little island there stood a lion, a magnificent maned creature whose pale pelt gleamed under the moon. The lion was pacing and turning around on the island as though in a cage. Several times he made as if to cross the water but withdrew as though from invisible bars. After a few minutes of this performance the creature flopped down disconsolately and lay with his head on his paws.

Somewhat reassured by the animal's apparent captivity, and also by some inner feeling which he could not put a name to, Rufus allowed his curiosity to draw him across and down the slope towards the spot.

—XIII—
Strange Encounters

RUFUS APPROACHED the lion rather as if in a dream. When he had come within hailing distance he paused, for the lion then turned its moist, languid eyes on him. For a moment Rufus wondered at his own temerity in coming so close to such a beast. The only lions he had seen before were those in the occasional circuses and shows of his native city. There was a difference, though, between looking at a caged beast and facing one in the wild across a few feet of naked space. Rufus comforted himself with the memory of the lion's strange and unsuccessful performance of trying to escape the narrow circle of water and then noticed again the dissatisfaction that lay behind the beast's wild grandeur.

Rufus approached the pool and walked around it, examining the unhappy beast curiously. The lion glanced at him a couple of times, stretched its cramped limbs and then rested its head on its paws with a sigh, gazing mournfully into the distance at nothing in particular.

'Poor creature,' said Rufus aloud after a while, 'I wonder what it is that keeps you cooped up there?'

The lion raised its head and looked at him quizzically for a moment before lowering it again.

'It can't just be the water,' continued Rufus musingly. 'Why I could quite easily step across it myself.'

'Ah, but it is the water,' said the lion in a deep, rumbling voice.

Rufus stepped back in astonishment and not a little alarm, almost tumbling backwards down the slope below the level space in doing so. A hint of amusement twinkled in the lion's eyes, but then he winced and stretched himself again as if to relieve a twinge of cramp.

Rufus looked all around himself cautiously, then turned again to the lion. 'That wasn't you speaking was it?' he asked.

'Why not?' growled the lion.

'Well, it's not usual for animals to speak, you know.'

The lion yawned. 'In this part of the world many things are usual which are accounted impossible elsewhere,' he said.

Rufus' consternation subsided a little and he walked around the island inspecting the lion with fresh interest.

'Why is it,' he asked at last, 'that you stay where you are when you seem so cramped and uncomfortable?'

'I'm like you,' replied the lion gruffly, 'I stay where I am because I cannot help it. Unlike you though, I know my misfortune. Also I know what needs to be done about it although I'm powerless to help myself. My real place is up there.' With his eyes the lion indicated the top of the hillock to the north of his island. 'If I could move there, I'd then have the freedom to go wherever I please.'

'What's preventing you then?' asked Rufus.

'As I said before, it's the water.'

'But what I mean is, what needs to be done to free you?'

'Why,' said the lion, looking at him almost slyly, 'if I had the help of a strong young man I could be free before this night is out.'

Rufus circled the pool and its island reflectively, wondering whether to take this hint. Though all this was rather unusual, strange enough things had happened already that night for him to adjust quickly enough to the situation. What he was wondering most in his perambulation was how much the lion was to be trusted, whether this was some kind of trick or not. The exact paths of his reasoning were not very clear even to Rufus, but somehow or other he came to a decision.

'Do you eat people?' he asked the lion at last. The lion laughed in a curious, rumbling sort of way.

'No master Rufus, I do not eat people. Not very often anyway.'

Rufus decided, however, that this last comment was in jest and said: 'Well then, what do you want me to do?'

The lion stretched, rose to his feet and looked Rufus closely in the eyes. 'You'll help me then?' he asked seriously. Rufus shrugged and nodded. 'It's not hard, what you have to do,' said the lion. 'Not very hard anyway, but you may be weary before you're through.'

'You said you could be free tonight,' said Rufus. 'Just tell me what needs doing and if I can help, I will.'

'Well, there are certain ways in which we must do these things,' said the lion. 'First we must realise in what way we are not free, then we must find out what needs doing to gain our freedom. Then, if we cannot do it alone, we must wait for one to come along and deliver us. It's most important to know exactly what needs doing before the deliverer comes along, otherwise they may only deliver us into greater bondage; but it's good to have help in gaining our freedom, it keeps us humble.'

Rufus did not exactly follow what the lion was talking about but he tried to look attentive. He suspected that his mask was seen through, however, because the lion suddenly changed his manner and became more businesslike.

'There's a spring here,' said the lion, nodding with his head at the southernmost point of the pool, the point where the water overflowed into a cleft and spilled out onto the slope of the mountain. 'There is also a channel running from here and circling the hill completely as this smaller one rings the island.

At least there was one but unfortunately it has been buried. If you were to clear it, the water would then flow out of this pool into it and I would be free to move to the hilltop.'

Thinking this a rather strange procedure, Rufus looked at the ground and saw that there were indeed traces of a channel which had once enclosed the whole area. 'But how am I to clear it?' he asked. 'The only tools I have are my bare hands.'

The lion then directed him to a sheltered place further down the mountainside. There he found the ruins of some small and simple dwelling by a spring, which perhaps was once a brave shepherd's hut or an anchorite's retreat. Amidst the ruin he unearthed an old spade, rather rusty and with a brittle handle, but nevertheless quite serviceable. He returned to the lion and set to work.

The sides of the channel were lined with roughly shaped stone and the earth within it was looser than that of the hillside, but even so Rufus soon began to doubt whether he could complete the work in a single night. It seemed to be the work of days at least. After toiling and sweating for a couple of hours, however, he began to suspect how it was to be done.

Looking up at the moon during a pause for breath, he realised that it had not moved an inch since the moment he had recovered from the impact of the dark phantom. He looked across at the lion and the lion returned his gaze with an expression of bland innocence. But if such a thing were possible, he was sure that around the lion's mouth there played a rather wily smile.

'Oh well,' thought Rufus, 'this is obviously not the night for questioning the strangeness of anything that happens, so I shall just have to make the best of it.' And he bent his back to the job again.

Exactly how long it took Rufus to clear the channel it is, of course, impossible to say, but while it lasted the work seemed to take days. He felt no need of sleep, however, and the only relief he took was an occasional drink and wash in the pool and a few minutes' rest in conversation with the lion. The beast had a fondness for obscure philosophy which, for the most part, Rufus could not follow; but whenever he sensed the failing of his listener's attention, the lion would switch the conversation to more commonplace matters. In these he revealed a pleasantly dry sense of humour and also that he knew all there was to know about Rufus' life and thoughts.

At last the job was complete. All that remained was to break the two thin walls separating the new channel from the old. Rufus leaned rather wearily on the stump of his spade and surveyed the trench with satisfaction. The soil neatly piled on its outer edge gave it something of the appearance of a small earthwork. The moon above was still riveted as fast as ever to its place in the bowl of the cloudless sky.

'Well, what now?' he asked.

'Rest yourself,' answered the lion, 'then when you are refreshed enough to appreciate it, you can let the water in.'

Rufus dipped his head into the pool again and took a drink, then he lay down against a soft mound of freshly-dug earth and relaxed. In a surprisingly short time his weary limbs ceased to ache and began to gather fresh strength. He wondered if it was something to do with the properties of the water.

As his limbs demanded less and less attention, so Rufus' curiosity re-awoke. At last he turned to the lion and said: 'Excuse me for asking, but who exactly are you?'

'Ah,' said the lion, 'I was wondering when you'd ask that. If you don't mind though, I'd rather keep it to myself for the moment. We share something in common, let's just leave it at that. But you must have almost recovered by now, come, let us finish the task.'

Rufus rose and broke the two remaining barriers. The water gushed into the new channel which, being deeper than the other, soon drained the pool. As soon as this happened, the lion sprang lithely off his island and stretched himself with all his feline strength; muscles rippling like steel cables, claws digging into the ground and tail lashing from side to side.

At this display of unchained animal strength Rufus shrank back instinctively, raising his spade as though it were a weapon and feeling glad he had remained outside the new ring of water.

His stretch completed, the lion turned to Rufus and, seeing his defensive posture, laughed merrily.

'Rufus my friend,' he said, 'you've done well so far tonight, don't make a fool of yourself now. You've nothing to fear from me and in your heart you know it. Come across and share with me my first view of new freedom.'

Feeling rather embarrassed, Rufus then laughed at his own fears. 'I'm sorry,' he said, 'I couldn't help myself. You probably don't realise how fierce you can look and how defenceless a man can feel unarmed in the presence of a lion. But a thought has just occurred to me; if you couldn't cross the water to get out, how am I to cross it to get in?'

'It's easy enough, my friend,' replied the lion. 'Just step across it. It's my water, not yours. Come on.'

Reassured, Rufus leaped lightly across the channel he had dug and joined the lion. As he approached, the lion held out his paw in greeting as a human would his hand. Rufus took it, stooping and then squatting on his heels to do so. This position they held for some moments, face to face and eye to eye in silent communion. Rufus had the peculiar feeling that a conversation was taking place between himself and the lion, but without his being conscious of what exactly they were talking about. He could feel an exchange of ideas going on, that he was learning something from the beast, but there were no words to express what it was he learned; unless it was that the lion, while having a lion's nature, was yet a far superior being to Rufus and possessed infinitely greater wisdom.

When the lion was satisfied, he turned away and together they climbed to the top of the little rounded hill.

Standing on top of the hillock, Rufus suddenly realised how remarkably well-placed it was for viewing the lands on either side and to the south. From everywhere else, in that region, the view was obscured by the peaks of the foothills, but from this position the peaks aligned themselves one behind the other like radiating pillars so that they interrupted the view as little as possible, almost as if they had been laid out with this deliberate intention. Rufus had looked around while working on the trench below, but had somehow not noticed this. He was as affected now as if in climbing the little hill they had scaled the mountain on whose flanks it stood. Under the moon and stars the world looked vast and breathtakingly beautiful. Far away to the south, Rufus fancied he could make out the isolated peak on which stood the City of Brown Gods. Without thinking, he put his hand on the lion's mane, as he would around the shoulders of a friend when sharing some great moment.

I fear I cannot quite do justice to this scene. It was as I have described it and yet there was something more which eludes words, some feeling in the air which gave everything its added vividness.

Rufus did not understand what was happening, he did not know how the lion could be confined by a mere stream or how this moving to the hilltop should free the beast, yet in accepting the lion's peculiar logic he now shared the animal's feelings and excitement. He did not understand the necessity for digging the trench and diverting the water into it, yet he now felt as proud of his work as if he had broken through the walls of a dungeon to free a friend. In the same way he now gazed out on the world with something of the lion's vision and exhilaration at being free, although he himself did not really know exactly why the lion was so much more free now than before. Beneath his fingers the lion's shoulders were quivering with excitement. Then the beast lifted his head and let out a wild, thundering roar of joy. This had a most unfortunate effect on Rufus' nervous system for his muscles melted to water and his bones, as once before that night, seemed to turn to jelly.

When the echoes died away and the whispering of the wind could once more be heard, the lion turned to Rufus apologetically. 'I'm sorry, my friend,' he said, 'I just couldn't resist it.' He paused and inspected Rufus critically. 'I've a feeling you must still be secretly rather afraid of me Rufus, or you would not scare so easily. But how could I even think of harming you after the favour you have just done me?'

Rufus' reaction, however, as before, was purely that of the instinct of man towards beast and this time he recovered more quickly. They turned and gazed out on the world again in silence. After a while Rufus asked thoughtfully: 'Then can you go where you like now?'

'Indeed I can,' came the reply, 'though in a sense part of me will always be here. I can go where I please but this hill is my home and wherever I go, I am at the same time still here. But enough of riddles my friend, the night wears on and you have more to do before it passes.'

Rufus glanced up into the heavens and saw that the moon had indeed now moved a little.

'But if it carries on at this rate,' he thought, 'I shall be an old man before sunrise.'

The lion then told Rufus that he was to go off into the mountains on their right, to the west. There he was to look for one in particular, whose shape he described carefully, and on this mountain he was to search out a particular cave. At that cave, said the lion, he would find an old friend who had something to show him. The friend would be sitting by a fire and this would make the journey easier because its light should be visible from far off, if he did not stray too far from his path.

'But come this way again,' said the lion, 'before returning to your city, for I wish to give you a token of my thanks and something to remember this night by. It's here, underneath this stone.'

The stone he seemed to be referring to stood upright on the very top of the hill. It was rough and slightly conical, about three feet high and a bit more than a span in thickness at the top.

After making his farewells, Rufus set off with a light heart through the gaunt foothills. Before passing out of sight he turned and waved to the lion who was lying majestically on his rounded hill like a monarch, glimmering in the moonlight. The only response to his wave was a swish of the beast's tail. Then Rufus turned and hastened into the west.

What a night of wonders this was! What a night to doubt the reality of everything about you, yet nothing yielded to his doubt. When he stumbled over loose rocks and boulders his shins felt no less painful for his doubts, his hands no less grazed. When he looked at the moon and defied its snail-like progress it moved no more quickly. 'And how can I be dreaming,' he wondered, 'when I can remember all my life up to this night as clearly as ever? They said rightly when they called this place haunted.' Yet there was no trace of apprehension in his heart and no nightmarish fears beset his imagination.

After several miles' journeying through shadowy gullies and past stony outcrops, Rufus spied a tiny red flame flickering against a patch of deep shadow on a mountain ahead. It beckoned him like a friendly beacon. The mountain stood out clearly against the deep, blue sky and its shape was exactly as the lion had described it. Rufus did wonder, for a moment, why the lion had been so meticulous in his description when the flame alone was enough of a guide, but this question was soon pushed aside by thoughts of who this old friend could be.

The fire was about a third of the way up the mountain on the face of a deeply-fissured cliff. The cliff leaned backwards slightly and, as he approached its foot, the fire disappeared from view, but he glimpsed it every now and then through cracks and clefts as he climbed. Without this beacon the climb would have taken many times as long as it did, for it was difficult to keep a steady path up the convolutions of the rock and several times he had to change his course drastically to avoid missing the place.

The climb itself was not too difficult, although the mountain rose steeply on this face. Time and the elements had cracked and cleaved the rock deeply and the vertical faces he had to tackle were seldom more than about fifteen feet in height, also they were plentifully patterned with hand and foot-holds. Even one with less climbing experience than that which Rufus had picked up in his youth would have found it quite easy, and without much incident he eventually pulled himself up over the lip of a ledge to find himself at his destination. With the upper part of his body on the ledge and his legs dangling over the drop behind, he paused to measure up the situation.

The ledge was about twenty feet wide. In the face of the cliff beyond it, gaped the mouth of a cave, like a tall, lop-sided Gothic arch. To the left of the cave's mouth burned the merry fire which had been his guide and beside that, with its back to a large square boulder and facing slightly away from Rufus, sat a figure on a rock; a slim figure in a black-hooded robe whose hand, in the act of putting a branch on the fire, was worn with age. The figure turned towards him with a smile. Two blank eyes like glistening pearls gazed in his direction, the eyes of the old blind lady from the city of Rufus' birth.

With a cry of astonishment, Rufus scrambled fully onto the ledge and across the space to her side. Taking her slim, delicate old hand in his he exclaimed: 'Why mother, what on earth are you doing here?'

'Hello, Rufus my son,' said she. 'I see you wasted no time in getting here.'

Rufus was lost for words. Several times he began to speak, but no coherent sentence escaped his lips.

'Come, my child,' said she. 'Sit on the ground here beside me and watch the flames for a while. Then when your mind is clear we shall talk.' He did as he was told, while she tossed a few more sticks into the flames from a small store beside her.

After a while they began to talk, with many questions on Rufus' side about how she came to be there and what connection she had with the lion and what was the explanation for the strange events of that night and so on. But to these questions the old woman simply smiled enigmatically and asked him instead to tell her about himself and all that had befallen him since the time they had met before. Since she doubtless knew already all that she wanted to know about him, this request was perhaps merely a device to get the conversation flowing in the way she wished. If so, her plan seemed to succeed, for Rufus, seeing that he would receive no answers to his own questions, until he had done so, gave in and began to give an account of his adventures since leaving home. In doing so he gradually calmed down and was soon speaking as easily as if this meeting on a forsaken mountainside, in the middle of the wilds, were the most natural thing in the world. Or almost so anyway for after a while, following a thoughtful pause, he said:

'But what puzzles me most is how to know whether or not I'm dreaming at the moment. I know that everything is different from usual this night and yet,' here he held up his grazed and blistered hands thoughtfully, 'and yet the night remains as real as ever. And here you are, but is it really you or are you no more than a shadow of someone I once met? It's the same as that other night, the one I told you about when the statue moved and spoke, I never could quite decide whether that was real or not.'

'Is it so important?' asked the old lady. 'Surely the important thing is not so much whether it is a dream, or a vision, or the normal daytime world, but whether we make the most we can of the situation and how much we learn from it. Though men may think dreams to be no more than delusions, this need not be so since the day is as full of illusion as the night. It's important to avoid snares and delusions, but this is as true of the day as the night. Truth may be found in either place as easily as falsehood. Listen, and I will try to make it clearer.

'In a dream it is often only a small part of you that lives and acts in the way you remember afterwards, yet it is still a part of your being. If you dream that you do something that, let us say, shocks you deeply when you wake in the morning, it solves nothing to say "but it was only a dream, I would never really do that" and then simply put it from your mind, because it was a part of you that did do it. If you just push it from your mind you are then living an illusion because in the full light of the sun that same part of you could act in the same way again, given the chance. So where then lies truth and illusion? If you had said "I see that if I were unfortunate enough to be put in the same situation as in my dream, I might be tempted to repeat those actions," then you will have learned something. Then you will have gained a little in truth.

'But these dreams in which a mere splinter of our being wanders, they slip easily from the mind for that very reason. When strange adventures befall you, which stay fully in the mind, why then, you can be sure that your whole being was involved and you can measure their importance by that standard. To question at the time whether you are asleep or awake or which sphere of existence you are in is to miss the point and to waste your energies. Time will reveal such things but while the adventure is upon you, the adventure is all that is important. When you met the lion it was not important for you to know whether or not you were dreaming, all that mattered was how you dealt with him. If you had made the wrong choice it would affect you no less if the choice were made in a dream or what you call the real world, and to what extent this night is a dream will become clear to you in time.'

Rufus mused on the lady's words for a while. They made him slightly uncomfortable because he preferred his own more practical view of the world to the rather fluid one suggested by the old lady which, if he took it too seriously all at once, seemed likely to lead into vast quagmires of confusion rather than clarity. Still, he had changed much since their first meeting and for her sake he felt happy enough to treat this night like any other, and to save the further implications of her words for future thought.

'Tell me about the lion then mother,' he asked after a while. 'Who is he and why did he need my help?'

The old lady laughed. 'He needed your help less than you suppose Rufus, you could help or hinder him about as much as you could the wind. It's more the other way round. Let me see now, how can I put it?'

'It's as he said, you and he have something in common. Or rather, you have something in common with him. Some part of you shares his lion's nature and your meeting was, if you like, a kind of test to see if you could recognise it. In sensing that he was more than simply a wild lion, in trusting your intuition enough to approach him instead of running away, you showed that you did recognise it even if at the time it seemed that your courage came mainly from his seeming to be trapped. What followed was like a kind of mime in which your positions were reversed. It was not he who was trapped on that little island, but rather that part of you which you share with him that is trapped in a similar way.

'In freeing him to return to his hill you were acting in mime the freeing of yourself. Yet it was only a mime, you are still in that particular state and your real freedom will only come some time in the future, more slowly but with no less effort than the digging of a trench. It was, if you like, a trial or dress-rehearsal, for if you hadn't done what he asked of you, what hope would you then have of freeing yourself in the same way?

'When we met before you were also being tried and that is why I say it matters less whether you are asleep or awake than whether you do the right thing. What hung in the balance tonight was no less important than that other time, when, for a while, your life was at risk.'

'Enough mother,' protested Rufus in light-hearted exasperation. 'Though you answer some of my questions you raise at least as many more in their place, my head is spinning. You tell me that it was not the lion I was freeing but some part of me which shares his nature, or something like that, but what part is it? I've felt no lion inside me before.'

The old lady laughed again merrily, then said: 'But even if it were possible to answer all your questions Rufus, so that none were left in your mind, would you really have me do it? Where then would be the challenge of finding the answers yourself?'

'Well,' said Rufus, 'maybe you're right. But I have another question in mind and if I may, I'll try my hand again in the hope of a simple answer. Tell me, was it you who whispered to me earlier tonight, at the beginning of all this, that I must turn and face that horde of phantoms? It was a woman's voice and I recognised it, but there was no time then to place who it was.'

'No,' replied the old lady, 'it was not me, but look into the fire and you'll see who it was.'

Rufus looked into the flames which danced around the dry branches. In the heart of the fire there hovered some blue flames and as he watched they grew and flared. The red flames, too, grew and changed their shape and the shadows in the embers shifted and settled themselves in new patterns. Gradually there formed before Rufus' eyes the head and shoulders of another woman, a younger woman than his companion, whose features were as distinct as if the fire were a window beyond which she stood. Her hair was silvery, almost white, and her robe was blue.

'Why,' exclaimed Rufus, half rising to his feet, 'that's one of the women who came for my table!' And indeed, the face in the flames was an exact likeness of Nuoma's.

'Come,' said the old lady when the picture had faded. 'I've something to show you which may lend weight to what I've been saying tonight, for it's only as a result of your actions that you're to see it. If there's time, we can talk some more afterwards.'

So saying she rose and, bidding Rufus to bring a couple of brands from the fire as torches, she led the way into the cave.

Rufus selected a couple of stout branches from the pile by the fire and poked the end of one of them into the flames. Rather to his surprise it burst immediately into life and, when he withdrew it, continued to flame strongly, defying the wind and burning more like a torch of tar-soaked rope than a brand of wood. The flame burned brightly but seemed to hardly consume the wood. Thinking again what a strange night this was, Rufus hurried into the cave after the blind woman.

The cave kept roughly the shape of its mouth, but narrowed as it entered the mountain and the floor sloped upwards. The floor was littered with bat droppings and other animal debris but the cave was quite empty at the moment. At the back was a rough natural stair just before the point where it seemed to come to an end. Climbing the steps, however, they found a passage beyond a jutting shoulder of rock, a narrow passage sloping down and slightly to the left into the heart of the mountain.

Squeezing past the shoulder, they went on in the face of a chill breeze rising from the depths. Needing no light, the old woman led the way swiftly and surely. Rufus followed more awkwardly, stumbling at times on the uneven floor and bruising his shoulders from time to time against the walls. In this manner they went on for some time with the breeze gradually growing warmer and the torch gradually shortening. Their way was fairly direct and though they passed a few passages branching off from their own, these were few enough not to cause any great confusion; and if Rufus had been abandoned down there, he could probably have found his way out again without too much difficulty, even without the aid of his torch.

Throughout the journey they spoke not a word. The old woman was no more than a black form hurrying silently on ahead of him and merging rather disturbingly at times with the dancing shadows cast by his torch. As they walked, Rufus thought how similar she and the lion were, not only at the moment, but when he had met her before also. They both seemed to know all about him and, for that matter, anything else they cared to know. Also they shared the same habit of talking in riddles.

At last, when the flaming brand had burned three parts of its length, the passage broadened, the roof climbed and they found themselves in the first of a series of caverns. The old woman stopped and turned to Rufus:

'Well, Rufus,' she said, 'here we are. Here is what I have to show you.'

Rufus looked around rather blankly. Ahead of them the caverns stretched away into the gloom beyond the reach of his torch. From the walls nearer at hand its light was reflected from the glistening surface of the rock which was punctuated by fantastic, wavering shadows. The lady smiled at Rufus' puzzlement.

'It had occurred to me,' she said, 'that you are in a rather helpless position at the moment, being a puppet king, isolated from your people. Our friend Aznavor will be sure to do all he can to keep matters like this, but though you're no match for his cunning and knowledge, you do have a few advantages on your side. For one thing, he dares not reveal his plans too much at the moment, and for another, you have me on your side to even the balance a little. So, if you're to free yourself from his control, if you're to begin to undo the evil plot he's been hatching, you must first win the hearts of your people. Then, if he suspects that you're a danger to him, he'll not dare to act too openly against you. Since on the whole most people's hearts are moved most easily by gold, it seemed to me that the simplest way of doing this would be for you to bring some of it with you to enrich your city. There are dangers in this, of course, but we'll speak of them later. Come over here and you'll see what I mean.'

The old woman led him over to their right and had him hold up his torch to the rock wall. There, from beneath the glistening moisture, was reflected a harder, metallic glint. Cutting across the wall like careless swathes of yellow paint swept broad veins of pure gold, sloping down at an angle into the floor.

—XIV—
Dreams that Stay Fully in the Mind

In silence, as on their way down, they returned to the mouth of the cave. Finding that the fire had fallen into a heap of glowing embers, they spent a while building it up again and then, after they had settled themselves, the old woman continued speaking.

'There are two conditions attached to this gift,' she said. 'The first is the most important, because if you stick to it you will avoid most of the dangers I mentioned earlier. If not, you'll find everything running out of control. I'll spell these conditions out carefully for you, because they will be no less binding when you have a mound of gold piled in your vaults, than they are now when it is still buried in the mountain. People will promise much when a gift is being offered them, but will often be tempted to take their vows less seriously when the thing is in their possession, thinking foolishly that whether or not they keep their promise can no longer affect them. So listen carefully. You may have cause to remember my words, if not as a timely caution then as a bitter reproach when it's too late.

'The first condition is this: that you shall not own any of the wealth that comes from this mine yourself, except in name. As king you already have more wealth and luxury at your disposal than you need, so leave this alone. This gold is purely for the benefit of your people, for you it's a means, not an end. If you can use it to benefit your city, that's all to the good, but in itself it cannot produce the changes that are needed. You'll have to remember the reasons I showed it to you and also that it was me who led you to it, then perhaps you'll find it easier to bear in mind that you do not own it, but are simply a kind of steward looking after it.

'The second condition is that you must not let any of it fall into the hands of Aznavor. This is why you'll have to claim it in your own name or rather, in that of the kingship. If you just try to give it to your people it will have to be done through the lords, and Aznavor being the chief of them will be free to help himself as he pleases and use it for his own ends. So claim it in the king's name and reserve to yourself the right to dispose of it. Then find a way to spend it as soon as you can and in such a way that as many of your people benefit as possible. Don't let it pile up for too long, for the pride of possession creeps subtly into the soul and the possession of gold most of all.

'You probably don't need telling this second condition, but it does no harm to say it. There will be times when you'll find it hard to resist Aznavor's pressure, when it will seem safer and wiser to give in to his demands for a share of it. This is why I make it a condition of the gift that you do not. It will make it easier for you to resist him then and will save you much heart-searching.

'You have many temptations ahead of you, for all will praise you for the finding of this wealth and few will question your right to spend it as you will. So take care. Take care also for the enmity of Aznavor. This will come as an unexpected distraction to his plans and, as your popularity and influence grow, he'll watch you closely for any sign of a threat to his power. So play the innocent and don't provoke him till you are ready. For both your own sake and your city's you must bring about his ruin in the end, but keep your intentions secret as long as possible. Make your plans in secret and share them only with your closest friends. Even then you must take care only to talk of them when you know Aznavor to be busy, for he has ways of overhearing which you little suspect.

'But that's enough of these matters my child,' she said, relaxing. 'I can give you no further advice or guidance that will be of much use, you'll just have to take things as they come. You agree though to abide by my two conditions?'

'Certainly,' replied Rufus readily, 'but what you say makes me realise mother, that I've not really thought very deeply about my position at all. I'm afraid I've only really been thinking about myself, about my own safety and survival. I have had a few thoughts about taking on Aznavor, but I've a feeling they were no more than daydreams. I think I only indulged myself in them because I felt my life to be in no immediate danger. You make me realise that I'm responsible for more than my own life now, that I'm responsible for the well-being of the people of the brown gods. I don't know or understand them, I don't feel like one of them and I'm sure that I'm the last person on earth that should be their king, yet despite it all perhaps I do have a duty towards them since I do find myself king. But the question is, am I capable of doing any more than saving my own skin?' He looked enquiringly at the old woman in black. She smiled kindly and replied:

'Well, who can tell, Rufus, until you've been put to the test? You can but do your best and you never know, but with a bit of luck that may be enough. Deal with things as they come, be cautious and you stand as good a chance of success as anyone in your position. But there's something else I wanted to ask you, Rufus. Tell me, what has become of Sophia, the last king's wife?'

This question caught Rufus rather off-balance, partly because of the abrupt change of subject and partly because he had hardly given Sophia a thought since the contest. Even then it had never occurred to him to find out where she had been taken by the palace guards.

'Why,' he replied, feeling somehow guilty, 'I haven't the faintest idea, mother. I've neither seen nor heard of her since they made me king. She tried to kill me you know, as revenge for King Gamil's death.' He frowned uncomfortably as memories of that time rose afresh in his mind. 'I can't say I've ever blamed her for it, but I'm afraid I've never really thought further about her.' He shifted restlessly on the rock which was his seat and was about to speak again when the old lady silenced him by resting her hand on his head.

'Hush, Rufus, say no more. What's done is done, you could have acted no differently unless it were to lose your life and who could have expected that of a young bantam like you? If the memory of that day troubles your conscience, seek out Sophia and see she comes to no harm. Make what amends you can for the troubles she has undergone and give her freedom to go where she wishes. That is all the debt you owe her. Now we have talked enough. Draw closer and rest your head on my knee. It's time you slept a while.'

Rufus rested his head on her knee and gazed into the flames while she stroked his temples and hair. They were surrounded by darkness now, for the moon had passed beyond the top of the cliff above them. The hills to their right were still brightly lit, but their own mountainside was in shadow. Rufus was wondering, vaguely, how he was to find his way down again when a sweet feeling of peace and drowsiness crept over him. His eyes grew heavy and within a few moments he was fast asleep.

He was roused by someone shaking him roughly by the shoulder and woke to find himself lying on a sloping hillside in the morning sun. His limbs were cramped and aching, his body studded with pain from the stones on which he lay. Dazed, he raised himself on his elbows to find that it was Shasta who had woken him. On his other side sat Nalna wearing a concerned expression, and over their shoulders he saw a small group of soldiers who had been in conversation, but were now all staring at him.

The morning was at that point where the first bright freshness of dawn begins to give way to the heat of the day, when the heat-haze begins to rise from the ground and the crickets to sing, but as yet all colours and forms are clear and distinct, and the heat still pleasant. The yellow and brown slopes on which he lay were those where the adventures of last night had begun. A little way to their left was the clump of rocks from which Rufus had leapt desperately into the phantom horde. The place where he lay was the spot where he had collided with the grinning, bulbous shadow.

'Why,' said Rufus aloud, 'then it was all a dream.'

At this sign of life, the faces of those around him relaxed with relief. Among the soldiers there were a few smiles and comments and then they withdrew further off to give him peace to recover properly.

'My lord,' said Shasta earnestly, 'you don't know how glad I am to hear you speak. For half an hour now we've been trying to wake you without success, until we began to think you must be bewitched or something.'

Rufus sat up, stretched himself and examined Shasta's face with curiosity. 'Why, Shasta, if I didn't know you better, I'd say you were betraying something like affection in your manner.'

'Don't mock me my lord,' said Shasta agitatedly. 'If you'd seen how close to death you looked, you'd not make fun of me so.'

Hearing this, Rufus sobered up a little, noticing that Shasta had called him 'my lord' twice in as many breaths and almost as if he meant the words.

'I'm sorry,' he apologised. 'Here, shake hands Shasta, and you Nalna. You don't know how glad I am also to see you again.' So the three of them shook hands and exchanged greetings like friends meeting at the end of separate journeys, which I suppose was more or less the case. Then they sat quietly for a while, alone with their various reflections. After they had rested like this, Nalna and Shasta reconstructed the events of the previous night from their own and the other soldiers' points of view, telling the story to Rufus between them. They were clearly more interested in anything Rufus had to say, but for the moment he thought it best to keep his own adventures to himself.

It seems then, that when Rufus had met with the grinning shadow and fallen briefly into unconsciousness, to the onlookers there was a blinding flash of lightning followed by thunder, howling wind and utter darkness which threw them into complete panic. Seized by madness, the men ran blindly in any direction, trying to escape the monsters they imagined to be about to leap on and devour them. They ran until they collapsed from exhaustion or had beaten themselves senseless against the mountain's rocks.

After a time the darkness had lifted and the wind died to a whimper. The storm clouds dispersed without shedding their rain and the moon swamped the hills with her light.

Then one of the trumpeters, finding himself alive and unharmed apart from the injuries he had done to himself in his panic, and meeting with a couple of fellow soldiers in a similar state, summoned the courage to blow a rallying-call on his bugle. Slowly and singly, the sorry company gathered around him in the valley like the last survivors of a conquered army. Not all turned up, but in fact they were surprised at the number who did, for running madly in the pitch dark in that place where crevasses, pits and cliffs abounded seemed the quickest way any of them could have looked for a speedy death.

In fact, as it later turned out, not one of their company had perished that night, and those who did not rally to the trumpet were scattered alive about the foothills, but were immobilised by twisted and broken limbs or trapped in pits. But I'm jumping ahead of the story here, for the missing men were not found till later.

Three parts of the company then, gathered about the bugler in the valley, at the foot of the mountain on which they had camped earlier. Among their number were Dornil, their commander, Shasta and Nalna. Dornil had been shaken and unnerved by the events, but he took command, and began to organise the men and try to count the missing. Shasta appeared to be in a state of shock, for he would not say a word and the expression in his eyes and movements was like that of a sleepwalker. Nalna was in much the same state as the rest of the soldiers, that is, one of confusion and fear, and possessed by a desire to get as far away from the place as possible.

Now, the men welcomed this reunion and having Dornil in command of them again, but what they most wanted was for him to command them to leave the place immediately. 'For,' they said, 'those who haven't come yet are unlikely to still be alive and if we don't make the most of this lull, who knows, but that we may all lose our lives yet tonight in a second assault.'

Dornil himself was more than half inclined to do just what they wanted, but the thought of the missing men who may yet be alive made him hesitate. And when he found that Rufus, their king, was among the missing, he knew that it was their plain duty to stay and search, if only for his body. The story then came out; how Rufus was last seen, apparently attacking the host of demons single-handed, just before the terrible darkness had fallen. Dornil then told them all that they would have to return to that place to look for any traces there might be of the king, but there was not enough authority and confidence in his voice to override the men's fears. For a while it seemed that mutiny was about to break out, some refused flatly with the fiercest oaths to ever go near the place again, others were less open but edged away as if making ready to desert if they could not win over their commander.

As has been said, Shasta all this time appeared to be in a state of shock. When the eyewitness account of Rufus' last actions came to his ears, however, he gave a start and comprehension seemed to return to his eyes. He looked around and listened for a while to the argument on all sides, and to Dornil's vain attempts to control the men. Then he came to life with an anger and force which shook them all, berating them for lily-livered cowards, unwilling to lift a finger to find the king when it was their king who had saved them all that night; how they must be blind not to see that it was Rufus' action which had completely scattered the ghosts and demons, for had any of them seen one since that moment? And had any of them come to any harm except by their own doing?

So Shasta railed at them, walking round and round the company and thus shepherding them into a tight knot, waving his sword and raging until they were not sure which they feared more, him or a host of phantoms.

While doing this, Shasta was not quite as hot-tempered as he must have seemed, because he had carefully selected a number of men who seemed more stout-hearted than the rest. At the end of his tirade he then turned to Dornil and offered his services to lead a party up onto the mountain to search for Rufus. So it was agreed. Shasta led his men away, leaving Dornil organising the remainder into search parties for the other missing, and agreeing to meet later at that same spot in the valley. The soldiers were now as docile as lambs, shamed by Rufus' bravery as presented to them by the old sergeant and by the memory of their own panic and fear. They were perhaps also encouraged by the fact that the sky in the east was now beginning to pale and the stars there to fade.

This, then, is the gist of the night's events as told to Rufus by Nalna and Shasta. This also was how Rufus woke that day to find himself already a bit of a hero even before he breathed a word of his actual experiences. He did not fully realise yet how much his status had changed, however, and he expected Shasta's strange deference to wear off before long.

'Well my lord, this is our side of the story,' said Shasta. 'But you've said nothing yet of your own part. Won't you tell us now?'

'Yes, Rufus,' joined Nalna. 'Don't keep us in suspense.'

Rufus said nothing for a while, but gazed thoughtfully out through the gaps in the mountains at the plain to the south. The events of the night before stood clearly before his mind; the lion, the old woman and the cave full of gold. He was thinking in particular of the woman's words about dreams that stay fully in the mind and the truth in them. He supposed that it had all been some kind of dream, if only for the fact that his hands were no more blistered and worn now than they had been before the flight down the mountainside. He supposed his body had lain here on the slope all night and that he had dreamt or imagined all that had happened. The memories, however, were as clear, if not more so, as those of the battle the day before. 'So if she's right,' he thought, 'there's truth in it, but what kind of truth we can only tell by going to see.'

While listening to his friends' accounts it had not escaped his notice that lower down the mountain, on its southern flank, was a level space in the centre of which rose a small, rounded hill. Turning to Nalna and Shasta he said:

'I'll tell you everything, my friends, but not yet. There are a few things I have to make sure of first. It will mean us making a bit of a journey, but it should not take more than a few hours to settle the matter.'

'You want us to go alone?' asked Shasta.

'Yes.'

'If you'll pardon my saying so, I think it would be wiser to take some of the company yonder with us,' said Shasta, nodding in the direction of the group of soldiers nearby.

Rufus was about to object, but looking at Shasta he then realised fully how great a strain the night must have been on the man's nerves. Shasta it was who, before the onslaught, had been trying to rally the men with the force of his own complete scepticism about ghosts and haunting, so how much greater must the terror of the phantoms have been to him. Looking then at Nalna, Rufus could not fathom the state of his mind at all. Now the tale of last night was told, the lad was quiet and reserved again. He did not seem much the worse for the night's events, but it seemed as if there was something he wanted to say but was holding back for some reason. Seeing that his friends also had their unresolved feelings, Rufus yielded to Shasta, saying: 'All right, but we need take no more than three men with us. Let the rest remain here and send word to Dornil that when we return, we shall all go down and join him.'

So it was arranged and Rufus and his five companions set off in search of the cave of his dream. On the way, remembering the lion's last words, Rufus stopped at the little hill on the level space.

This was much as he had seen it before, except that there were no rings of water. On the south side, however, there was a small spring whose waters trickled a short way down the slope before losing themselves among the rocks. Also there were slight traces on the ground as if there could once have been a trench encircling the hill, though Rufus thought it might just be his imagination that suggested this.

Climbing to the top of the little hill, they found that the view to the south was in fact remarkably open from there, and that the peaks of the foothills did align themselves like pillars radiating from that spot. At the very top of

the hill stood an upright stone about three feet tall. With not a little effort they managed to dislodge this and, putting his hand into the hole thus left, Rufus withdrew from it a heavy bronze medallion on a stout chain. The face of the medallion bore a design which seemed at first to be of the sun, but on closer inspection revealed itself to be the head of a lion whose mane radiated like the sun's fires.

This performance greatly excited the curiosity of Rufus' companions, especially the finding of the medallion under a stone which had clearly not been disturbed since time immemorial. When he hung it around his neck below the amethyst cross, they looked at him expectantly for an explanation, but all he said was: 'Patience, my friends, we're not finished yet.'

Nalna and Shasta exchanged a meaningful glance, for although he was unconscious of it, Rufus had acquired a new dignity overnight, a quiet authority, which he had not possessed before. This had nothing to do with the new respect in which he was held, for of that he was not yet fully aware.

Leading his companions into the hills to the west, Rufus realised that this was why the lion had described the mountain with its cave so carefully to him last night. The way was just as he remembered it and this, together with the finding of the medallion, led Rufus to expect quite confidently that the gold, too, would be where he had dreamt it. Since he also remembered the old woman's injunctions, Rufus did not get too excited over the prospect of the discovery, but he had after all been a merchant's apprentice trained from childhood in the ways of dealing with wealth, so he could not prevent a faint fluttering of his insides at the thought of having so much of it at his command.

In time they came to the mountain and, leaving the three soldiers on guard at its foot, Rufus led the way up the cliff-face following the route he had used the night before. He knew this way zig-zagged rather wildly up to the cave and made the climb longer than it need be, but decided this was better than trying a more direct route and possibly missing the cave. So up they went.

Rufus and Nalna both had fair heads for heights and so forgot that Shasta might not find it so easy. Shasta in fact had no head for heights at all, but he was not going to be shown up again by either of his former pupils so, saying nothing and gritting his teeth grimly, he doggedly followed in Rufus' tracks, his eyes glued firmly on the nimble pair of heels above him.

After about half an hour's climbing they gained the ledge and the cave. There they rested for a while in the open to catch their breaths before entering. As they were about to go in though, Rufus stopped with a frown and a stifled oath.

'What's wrong?' asked Nalna.

'I never thought to bring a light,' answered Rufus, looking down at the ground to the left of the cave's entrance where the fire had been last night. He supposed he must have been expecting to find the remains of the fire to use for light, but if he'd only thought about it he knew he would not have counted on doing so. Especially not on finding wood that would make such good torches as those he had used last night, since that must have been some of the old lady's doing. 'That will teach me to daydream on the way here,' he thought.

'If you'd told us where we were going, we might have thought of it for you,' commented Shasta with a touch of his usual irony.

'Oh well,' said Rufus rather ruefully, 'we may as well look as far as we can.'

The cave was as he remembered it, narrowing as it went in and the floor sloping gently upwards. Now, however, it was full of bats who clung twittering and restless to the roof rather like clusters of grapes, disturbed by the noise of their entrance. At the back of the cave, where last night a shoulder of rock had hidden the passage leading down into the mountain, their way was blocked almost to the roof by a tumbled wall of small boulders. Climbing up to the gap at the top, Rufus found a chill breeze whistling out from the passage beyond.

'Well I think it's all right,' said Rufus scrambling down again. 'I don't think this wall is very thick but the question is, how long would it take to break through it and what can we do about light if we were to manage it?'

'You'd still rather not tell us what we're looking for yet?' asked Shasta.

'Well . . .' began Rufus, but seeing his hesitation Nalna made a suggestion.

'The men we brought with us,' he said, 'were carrying their packs. I wouldn't be surprised if one of them had a lantern and kindling.' Shasta then eyed the rough wall critically and said:

'If we were to clear a hole through the wall while you went down for a lamp, would that still leave us enough time to find whatever it is we're looking for?'

At this suggestion Rufus brightened up and, glancing out at the angle of the sun, agreed that it would leave them plenty of time. As he set off Shasta called out:

'Oh, Rufus.'

'Yes?'

'You might see if any of them has some rope.'

'What for?'

'You never know, we may find a use for it,' replied Shasta noncommittally.

Everything went well. Rufus found a more direct way down the cliff and back again, taking not much longer in the double journey than the three of them had on the way up. He returned with the lantern and rope to find that the other two had cleared a large enough gap for them to squeeze through. From then on everything was exactly as it had been in Rufus' dream and in the heart of the mountain they found the gold mine just as the blind lady had shown it to him.

Back on the surface again, sitting on the edge of the ledge and looking out into the afternoon, Rufus finally told them everything he had experienced the night before. Nalna and Shasta listened in amazement, and when he had finished could not at first find any comment to make. Finally it was Shasta who spoke. But if, a while before, he had begun to recover his normal easy-going manner towards Rufus, he now seemed to have relapsed into the same uncomfortable deference he had shown in the morning.

'You'll pardon me, my lord,' said Shasta, 'but when you were first assigned to me for training I little thought you had the makings of a king in you. Just a young pup you seemed to me then, though I did think that if you lived long enough something might be made of you. There seemed little chance of it at the time, with you entered for the contest, but I said nothing because it was none of my business. Shows how wrong a man can be. What I'm trying to say, my lord, is like an apology. It not being something I'm used to doing I can't find the right words, but I apologise. I've misjudged you. Aye and others have too, but last night you showed how wrong we all were. It was enough that you were the only one of us last night to keep your head and your courage, but now there's this as well. This dealing with spirits and lions, gods for all I know, and far from being the worse afterwards you come out of it with a mountain of gold to your credit.'

'That's more or less what I've been wanting to say also,' interrupted Nalna. 'I told you once Rufus, that I could not respect you as our king but only as a friend, but I judged you wrongly, I didn't know ...'

But Rufus could stand no more of this.

'Stop, stop my friends!' he cried almost in alarm. 'What are you trying to do to me? Do you want to puff my head up till it bursts? I'll have no more of it. I prefer you, Shasta, when you call me "young Rufus" and when in public you call me "my lord" as if it were the rank of one of the men in your command. This flattery suits you almost as little as it does me. And you, Nalna, you're my friend and know me well enough, so how can you misunderstand me so much and talk to me like this? You're my only two friends here, but when you "my lord" me like this you isolate me as much as when I first came here, more so in fact. Haven't you listened to what I've been saying? I did nothing last night from my own judgement and courage, I only did what I was told to do and had little choice in the matter. The lady told me I'd be tempted by flattery, but I didn't expect it so soon and least of all from you. If I can't make you see what really happened, you the only friends to whom I can speak my mind openly, who will I have to remind me of the truth later?'

'That's all very well to say,' said Shasta, 'but men judge others mostly by their deeds and the results they bring, so how can we but look on you differently now? If the Smiling One himself had told me last night to stand and face those devils, my legs would have kept on running the other way just as fast. Aye,' he frowned ferociously at the recollection. 'Aye, I would have kept running just as fast, so how can you expect me not to admire your courage for what you did? If it's as you say, if the witch who showed you the gold also warned you against the pride it might raise in you, then I should heed the warning, but it's a matter between you and your conscience. Me and young Nalna here can do little about it either way.'

'Shasta's right,' said Nalna. 'It's no good wishing that nothing has changed between us, because it has.'

'Then what am I to do?' asked Rufus. 'I need to feel I can talk to you as friends. I'll need it more in the future if your reactions to this gold are anything to go by, but you seem so distant from me now.'

He looked troubled and the others did not know what to say. As they sat in silence though, Shasta watched Rufus closely and seemed to be thinking hard about the situation, and with some success apparently, for in a while he said:

'For my own part Rufus, I'm not sorry for the change. I'm a sergeant, no more. It's no sadness to me to find that the king I serve is worthy of the name. But there's no reason why this should be the end of our friendship, or why you can no longer talk openly with us. If I can no longer treat you as one of the fledgelings I'm given to lick into shape, there's no harm in it. You're king after all, it's not fitting for a sergeant to patronise a king. If I admire your courage now, it doesn't mean the end of our friendship. What it means is that you've come of age, you're a man now and don't need me to father you any more. This day you've become king in truth not just title, so why fear that people will mistake you for one? You're the king, so what harm can it do to be seen to act like a king? If you think this means I'm going to flatter you for it, you should know better because I've never been one for kowtowing to my superiors and I'm not going to start now. As to what others will say of you after this day, well, so long as you don't feel too proud within yourself, let them say what they will. If the people want to praise and honour you, let them. The best way to look at a king is with a crick in the neck.'

Seeing that these words seemed to cheer Rufus up a little, he took a deep breath and continued with a bit of a grin; addressing Nalna although his words were meant for Rufus.

'But perhaps I spoke too much in haste, Nalna, when I said we could do nothing for Rufus and his pride. As loyal subjects which we now are, we're bound to do as he bids us. If he bids us keep him humble, maybe it's our duty to do so, hard though it may be for us. If we practise hard enough, perhaps we can learn to ply him with insults from time to time, purely as a matter of duty, much though it goes against the new-found respect we have for him. What do you say?'

'Why not?' rejoined Nalna, grinning also. 'If, as you say, it's a matter of duty, then we must do the best we can.'

Then Rufus laughed happily, saying: 'Why, that's the longest speech I've ever heard you make Shasta and I thank you for it. I feel much better, almost myself again.' And after more banter the friendship between them was restored completely. The pattern of their relationship had changed, however, because Rufus had now taken first place in their trio. Without his noticing it, the mantle of quiet authority which his friends had noticed earlier slipped again over his shoulders.

After a while he said: 'One of these days Shasta, you'll have to meet my friend, Lazarus. He once did me a similar service and I think you'll find you have much in common with him. Someone said once that life moves in a spiral way, I begin to see now how it is.'

'What plans do you have now?' asked Nalna a little later.

'Well,' said Rufus, 'on the way here a lot of ideas passed through my mind, but most of them, I think, were no more than daydreams, because so much depends on the way things turn out. So I haven't many plans yet, but first of all I want to set the carvers to work on a statue of the lion to go where I found this.' He touched the bronze medallion on his chest. 'Also, I want a pool made there to circle the hill as it was in the dream. When that's done we'll start work seriously on the mine.

'There's probably an easier way to get here than the way we came. Perhaps we can cut a road going straight to the south beyond the hills and then crossing the plain to meet the old road. We'll have to build a fortress of some kind nearby to guard the mine and the wagons taking the gold to the city. That should be enough to occupy our minds for the moment. There'll be time enough to decide what to do with the gold while these things are being done.'

As it was now a couple of hours past noon and they imagined that their men would all want to be as far as possible away from these hills by nightfall, they decided they had best return to the rest of their force. So, tied together with the rope, which Shasta was now not too ashamed to admit feeling happier with, they descended the cliff, joined the three soldiers at its foot and tramped briskly back towards the east.

—XV—
The King's First Judgement

PASSING THE little hill where the statue of the lion was to go, Rufus and his companions approached the place where he had been found that morning. Now, as we have seen, the arrangements were that the rest of Shasta's men were to await their return there, and then they were all to go on down into the valley to rejoin Dornil. As they approached the place, however, they found that Dornil and all his company, including the injured, had come up to meet them instead. The soldiers were sitting around in groups, talking and joking much as usual though there was an air of uncomfortable tension underlying their manner. Their packs and gear, salvaged from where they had been abandoned higher up the mountain, were piled in mounds between the groups. Dornil sat apart in morose contemplation. When he saw them coming he started to his feet and came quickly to greet them. An instant hush fell upon the rest of the assembly.

'What can be the meaning of this?' wondered Rufus aloud.

'I doubt if you'll have long to wait for an answer to that question,' said Shasta. 'See what a hurry young Dornil is in. Ho there, Dornil,' he called out, 'what's your rush? We'll be with you soon enough.'

Dornil, however, was in no mood for banter and ignored Shasta completely. In his face, as he approached, there was a genuine enough expression of relief at seeing Rufus alive and whole, but he was clearly also troubled about something.

When the greetings were made, Rufus asked the commander why he had brought all the men back up the mountain when their march lay in the opposite direction. He asked also why Dornil was troubled, had they lost many men that night or was it something else? Dornil hesitated, glancing at Rufus' companions and especially Shasta as if reluctant to speak in front of them, then said:

'Well, it's all to be done in the open my lord, so I'll hold nothing back. I was troubled, it is true, to hear that no sooner had you been found than you disappeared again into the wilds, but it was not for your safety that I feared. It seemed to me that if you had survived the night you had little to fear from the day. No, it was something else, it was the delay it meant before we could decide what it is that needs deciding. But come, what I have to say is for the ears of all the men.'

So saying, Dornil led Rufus over to the pile of rocks and asked him to be seated. Shasta sat on the ground to his right and Nalna on a low rock to his left. Dornil stood a little way off, lower down the slope, and beyond him were the soldiers arrayed lower down again. The men had raised a subdued cheer for Rufus' arrival and, like Dornil, their welcome was genuine enough but they, too, were tense and expectant, and the unease which had been latent before had now risen to the surface.

With the scene thus set, Dornil addressed Rufus in a clear, firm voice, speaking just loudly enough to be heard by all present.

'My lord,' he began, 'the reason we came here to meet you instead of waiting below is that before we leave these hills there are matters to be decided. As our king I ask you in the name of us all to judge for us how we stand after the events of last night. We came up to this place because it was fitting to return to the place where we were shamed in order to be judged. All of us, in some degree, have failed in our duty and betrayed our oaths of loyalty and so we ask you now to decide for us our penalty. All of us, that is, except you and,' here he paused and swallowed as if literally swallowing his pride, 'and sergeant Shasta who also put us to shame, for it was he who brought us to our senses again. If it were not for him we may well have left you and those of our comrades who were lost among the hills to perish out here, for in our fear we supposed you all dead. More, I think, because we wished to leave as soon as we could than for any other reason. But, whatever the reason, there can be no excuse for our wishing to desert you, especially since we have now found that none have lost their lives, though if we had abandoned them they would surely have done so.

'To you then we all owe our lives for putting the demons to flight, and to the sergeant we owe the lives of all those we would have left. The sergeant did what it was my place as leader to do, but I had not the power. So first, I ask you to judge the two of us, to decide his reward and my forfeit. Next, I ask you to judge us all, for all alike were soldiers who abandoned their king in the face of the enemy and that the enemy was from hell, not earth, can be no excuse for us.'

Dornil concluded his speech and looked around at the assembled company as if inviting anyone to add to what he had said, but none offered to do so. He then turned again to face Rufus and waited expectantly, proud and prepared to accept the worst with dignity.

Rufus, too, looked around at the faces of the subdued company and then at Dornil. For a moment a devil of his own was aroused by the situation, a devil whose promptings if put into words would sound something like: 'so here you are, Rufus. Here you sit and all these proud men now look up to you, hanging on your every word. They put their fates in your hands and will accept whatever they judge to be their due without a whimper. These men who so short a while ago merely tolerated your presence with no more than an outward show of respect, who were so proud of their own valour and laughed at your deeds in battle as they would on the first stumblings of a child, who looked on you as no more than a gaudy puppet, these proud men now bend their heads in obeisance to you. And why not, seeing how you did what none of them would have dared? Shall you not make it even more clear to them now how much they misjudged you?'

But as I said, it was only for a moment that this devil was roused and then Rufus recovered himself. He looked around the company again, wondering what to say. Nalna, beside him, seemed to have been reminded by Dornil's words of his own terror the previous night, he perched uncomfortably on his rock and would not meet Rufus' eyes. Shasta, too, had been reminded of his own failings, as he saw them, but his sense of humour had not failed to be tickled by Dornil's praise of him. In the light of the long-standing feud between them, such sweet words could not be passed over even at a time like this; but rather regretfully he decided he would have to tell Rufus that Dornil was doing himself an injustice by his words. He opened his mouth to say so, but Rufus stayed him with a motion of his hand and said quietly:

'You told me I should be seen to act as a king Shasta, so now I shall try.' Then turning to Dornil he said in a louder voice:

'You ask me to give judgement, well the task is not a difficult one, for it's already clear to me how I must decide. I've already been told of all that befell last night and in more detail than your commander has just done, so I've had time to think it over. I think you put your own actions in a worse light than others saw them Dornil, but perhaps you do this because the higher the duty a man has the more severely he's held to account for it. So perhaps the greater command shown by one of your sergeants would justify your ranks being exchanged, if it were not that the sergeant's courage was possibly helped by an inability to believe certain kinds of truth till they smack him in the face.' This was rather a fine stroke and Rufus was taking a chance both on Shasta's goodwill and his own understanding of the situation, but he was rewarded by a burst of surprised laughter from the men and even Shasta grinned.

'My own courage,' continued Rufus quickly, before his mockery of Shasta had time to turn sour, 'was rather like that of an animal going to the slaughter-house, whose courage springs largely from the hand that wields the pointed stick behind him. So if it's punishment you're wanting for the failure of your nerve last night, I should not look to me for it, for we're all equally guilty. Soldiers are not trained for fighting spirits or madness, so who can hold them guilty if they forget themselves and fly before them?

'But since you have asked for my judgement, I shall give it and let it be binding. My judgement then is this; that as to rank, order, precedence and position everything shall remain as it was this time yesterday. Your sergeant shall be no more than a sergeant and your commander no less than a commander, you men shall be no less than men-at-arms in the service of the City of Brown Gods. If you must give thanks for still having your lives today, then offer them to those kind spirits who helped me, your king, and whose strength was greater than that of the demons who assaulted us last night. There was not only evil walking these hills last night, and in time you'll see that the price we've paid in pain and fear is a small one for what we've gained today. But now, in case we should seem to be tempting fate, or at the very least to be tempting the strength of our nerves, I suggest we leave these hills and try to reach the road and the rest of our force before we camp for the night.'

So it was settled and all seemed to have their minds put at ease, if only because they were now more occupied in wondering what gain it was that Rufus had hinted at than in remembering their fear and the shame it had brought on them. If they did not take Rufus' words concerning himself quite literally, ascribing them to modesty on his part, they accepted the rest of what he said gladly, accepting whole-heartedly the absolution from failure of duty, which his judgement offered, and along with it the restoration of everyone's rank and station to what it had been before.

Shasta and Dornil, too, seemed to accept the judgement quite readily and as he marched along behind them, Rufus overheard them talking together in their usual manner, swapping insults and mockery in a gruff but good-humoured way. When alone their talk was as between equals and, curious about the relationship between the two, Rufus caught them up and eaves-dropped quite unashamedly.

'That was very noble of you Dornil,' said the sergeant, 'to praise me like that before all the men. If I didn't know you were playing on our king's soft heart I might have thought you'd finally realised where the worth lies between us.'

'You wouldn't recognise true worth even if it did hit you in the face, Shasta. You were ever the same, even when we were first in training. Whenever I came ahead of you you'd always have some excuse for why you didn't want to win. And when out of pity I'd sometimes let you, you'd always say it was your skill that did it. Sometimes, you know, I suspect that you still don't really believe that I'm a commander, because I've earned it while you're still a sergeant, because you fritter away your time and get drunk too often.'

'What!' cried Shasta. 'Who's this talking about true worth? You think I couldn't be a commander myself if I wanted? You think I couldn't take your place this minute if I cared to? But who wants to be a captain, always having to watch your men, both on duty and off, and never able to loosen up and relax of an evening in case you make a fool of yourself, which the best of us have to do from time to time in order to live. Who'd want to always be on duty, never free to go out on the town and clear out the system like any decent man needs to do? It's not even as if the money's worth it. Why, I can earn as much in an evening with the dice as you do in a week and what's more I can enjoy myself at the same time.'

'Except that you always lose it again the next night one way or another,' retorted Dornil drily. 'Just look at you, what have you got to show for all these years in the service? You still live in the barracks like you did when you first joined and I doubt if you've more than one coat besides the one the army gives you. Where's all this wealth you've made then while I've been scraping by on my wage?'

'Pah! What would I want with a fancy house like yours and the fancy wife that goes with it and won't let you stir a finger of a night without her permission. No, not even in her direction I shouldn't wonder. Give me a good tavern any time and a good fighting-wench for company. And if they're both mine for the night, what more could I ask for? I don't need to own them to enjoy them. Where's all my money gone you ask me? Into life my friend, that's where. And when we're both sitting toothless and witless in the sun at the end of our days, I wonder which of us will be the poorer?'

'Yes I wonder,' said Dornil. 'For I'd lay a bet on it that it will be my bench we're sitting on.'

So ended the incident in the haunted hills and so began a new chapter in Rufus' life, for it was only at this time that he can truly be said to have become king in the City of Brown Gods. Or perhaps, I should say, that he first began to be king, because it was only a beginning.

So also ends the first part of his story, showing how the cloth-merchant's apprentice became a king and how his involvement with the Golden Wheel began. Those who think this book too short and wish I'd carried the story further before stopping, well, I thank them for their interest and hope they will have the patience to wait with good humour for the next one, in which Rufus' tale will be continued. Those who think the story already more than long enough, I hope will thank me for thus relieving them of the rest of it.

In deciding to end this volume at this point, I have followed the advice of the sage who says 'A lake occupies a limited space. When more water comes into it, it overflows. Therefore limits must be set for the water.'